A MAN IN ...
AND ...
LADY INTO FOX

David Garnett was born in Brighton, Sussex, in 1892. After
studying botany at Imperial College, London, he returned to
Sussex as a conscientious objector, working on the land and
living at Charleston with the painters Duncan Grant and
Vanessa Bell. After the war he became increasingly involved in
the literary life of the capital: first as a bookseller, then a
partner in the Nonesuch Press and also as literary editor and
contributor to the *New Statesman*. He worked as a historian
for the government during World War II, but then returned to
publishing. He was made a CBE in 1952. His first book, *Dope
Darling*, was followed by twenty-two more works of fiction.
His nonfiction includes the translation from the French of the
edited letters of T. E. Lawrence (1938) and Dora Carrington
(1970).

After the death of his wife, Ray Marshall, David Garnett
married Angelica, the child of Duncan Grant and Vanessa
Bell. He spent his last years in France and died in 1981.

David Garnett

A MAN IN THE ZOO
AND
LADY INTO FOX

VINTAGE

Published by Vintage 2000

2 4 6 8 10 9 7 5 3 1

First published in Great Britain in one volume
by Chatto and Windus 1947

Vintage
Random House, 20 Vauxhall Bridge Road,
London SW1V 2SA

Random House Australia (Pty) Limited
20 Alfred Street, Milsons Point, Sydney,
New South Wales 2061, Australia

Random House New Zealand Limited
18 Poland Road, Glenfield,
Auckland 10, New Zealand

Random House (Pty) Limited
Endulini, 5A Jubilee Road, Parktown 2193, South Africa

The Random House Group Limited Reg. No. 954009
www.randomhouse.co.uk

A CIP catalogue record for this book
is available from the British Library

ISBN 0 099 28549 5

Papers used by Random House are natural,
recyclable products made from wood grown in sustainable forests.
The manufacturing processes conform to the environmental
regulations of the country of origin

Typeset by Deltatype Ltd, Birkenhead, Merseyside
Printed and bound in Denmark by
Nørhaven A/S, Viborg

A MAN IN

THE ZOO

TO
HENRIETTA BINGHAM
AND
MINA KIRSTEIN

AUTHOR'S NOTE

I HAVE TO thank Mr. Arthur Waley for permission to quote from his translation of a poem by Wang Yen-shou, which appears in 'The Temple and other Poems,' published by Messrs. Allen & Unwin.

I also wish to say that the Royal Zoological Society has always been the object of my respect and admiration, and that in this story, neither explicitly nor implicitly, is anything intended that could be regarded as derogatory to the Society in any sense.

A MAN IN THE ZOO

JOHN CROMARTIE AND Josephine Lackett gave up their green tickets at the turnstile, and entered the Zoological Society's Gardens by the South Gate.

It was a warm day at the end of February, and Sunday morning. In the air there was a smell of spring, mixed with the odours of different animals – yaks, wolves, and musk-oxen, but the two visitors did not notice it. They were lovers, and were having a quarrel.

They came soon to the Wolves and Foxes, and stood still opposite a cage containing an animal very like a dog.

'Other people, other people! You are always considering the feelings of other people,' said Mr. Cromartie. His companion did not answer him, so he went on:

'You say somebody feels this, or that somebody else may feel the other. You never talk to me about anything except what other people are feeling, or may be going to feel. I wish you could forget about other people and talk about yourself, but I suppose you have to talk of other people's feelings because you haven't any of your own.'

The beast opposite them was bored. He looked at them for a moment and forgot them at once. He lived in a small space, and had forgotten the outside world where creatures very like himself raced in circles.

'If that is the reason,' said Cromartie, 'I do not see why you should not say so. It would be honest if you were to tell me you felt nothing for me. It is not honest to say first that you love me, and then that you are a Christian and love everybody equally.'

3

'Nonsense,' said the girl, 'you know that is nonsense. It is not Christianity, it is because I love several people very much.'

'You do not love several people very much,' said Cromartie, interrupting her. 'You cannot possibly love people like your aunts. Nobody could. No, you do not really love anybody. You imagine that you do because you have not got the courage to stand alone.'

'I know whom I love, and whom I do not,' said Josephine. 'And if you should drive me to choose between you and everybody else, I should be a fool to give myself to you.'

DINGO ♂
Canis familiaris var.
NEW SOUTH WALES, AUSTRALIA

'Poor little Dingo,' said Cromartie. 'They do shut up creatures here on the thinnest pretexts. He is only the familiar dog.'

The Dingo whined, and wagged his tail. He knew that he was being spoken of.

Josephine turned from her lover to the Dingo, and her face softened as she looked at it.

'I suppose they have got to have everything here, every single kind of beast there is, even if it turns out to be nothing but an ordinary dog.'

They left the Dingo, walked to the next cage, and stood side by side looking at the creature in it.

'The slender dog,' said Josephine, reading the label. She laughed, and the slender dog got up and walked away.

'So that is a wolf,' said Cromartie, as they stopped six feet further on. 'Another dog in a cage . . . Give yourself to me, Josephine, that sounds to me as if you were crazy. But it shows anyway that you are not in love with me. If you are in love it is all or nothing. You cannot be in love with several people at once. I know because I am in love with you, and other people are all my enemies, necessarily my enemies.'

'What nonsense!' said Josephine.

'If I am in love with you,' Cromartie went on, 'and you with me, it means that you are the only person who is not my enemy, and I am the only person who is not yours. A fool to give yourself to me! Yes, you are a fool if you fancy you are in love when you are not, and I should be a fool to believe it. You do not give yourself to the person with whom you are in love, you are yourself instead of being dressed up in armoured plate.'

'Has this place got nothing in it besides tame dogs?' asked Josephine.

They walked together towards the lion house, and Josephine took John's arm in hers. 'Armoured plate. It doesn't seem to me to make sense. I cannot bear to hurt the people I love, and so I am not going to live with you, or do anything that they would mind if they found out.'

John said nothing to this, only shrugged his shoulders, screwed up his eyes, and rubbed his nose. In the lion house they walked slowly from cage to cage until they came to a tiger which walked up and down, up and down, up and down, turning his great painted head with intolerable familiarity, and with his whiskers just brushing the brick wall.

'They pay for their beauty, poor beasts,' said John, after a pause. 'And you know it proves what I've been saying. Mankind want to catch anything beautiful and shut it up, and then come in thousands to watch it die by inches. That's why one hides what one is and lives behind a mask in secret.'

'I hate you, John, and all your ideas. I love my fellow creatures – or most of them – and I can't help it if you are a tiger and not a human being. I'm not mad ; I can trust people with every feeling I have got, and I shall never have any feelings that I shouldn't like to share with everybody. I don't mind if I am a Christian – it's better than suffering from persecution mania, and browbeating me because I'm fond of my father and Aunt Eily.'

But Miss Lackett did not look very browbeaten as she said this. On the contrary her eyes sparkled, her colour was high and her looks imperious, and she kept tapping the toe of her pointed shoe on the stone floor. Mr. Cromartie was irritated by this tapping, so he said something in a low voice on purpose so that Josephine should not be able to hear it; the only word audible was 'browbeating.'

She asked him very savagely what he had said. John laughed. 'What's the use of my talking to you at all if you fly into a rage before you have even heard what I have got to say?' he asked her.

Josephine turned pale with self-control; she glared at a placid lion with such fury that, after a moment or two, the beast got up and walked into the den behind his cage.

'Josephine, please be reasonable. Either you are in love with me or else you are not. If you are in love with me it can't cost you much to sacrifice other people to me. Since you won't do that it follows that you are not in love with me, and in that case you only keep me hanging round you because it pleases your vanity. I wish you would choose someone else for that sort of thing. I don't like it, and any of your father's old friends would do better than me.'

'How dare you talk to me about my father's old friends?' said Josephine. They were silent. Presently Cromartie said, 'For the last time, Josephine, will you marry me, and be damned to your relations?'

'No! You silly savage!' said Josephine. 'No, you wild beast. Can't you understand that one doesn't treat people like that? It is simply wasting my breath to talk. I've explained a hundred times I am not going to make father miserable. I am not going to be cut off without a shilling and become *dependent* on you when you haven't enough money to live on yourself, to satisfy your vanity. My *vanity*, do you think having you in love with me pleases my *vanity*? I might as well have a baboon or a bear. You are Tarzan of the Apes; you ought to be shut up in the Zoo. The collection here is incomplete without you. You are a survival – atavism at its worst. Don't ask me why I fell in love with you – I did, but I cannot marry Tarzan of the Apes, I'm not romantic enough. I see, too, that you do believe what you have been saying. You do think mankind is your enemy. I can assure you that if mankind thinks of you, it thinks you are the missing link. You ought to be shut up and exhibited here in the Zoo – I've told you once and now I tell you again – with the gorilla on one side and the chimpanzee on the other. Science would gain a lot.'

'Well, I will be. I am sure you are quite right. I'll make arrangements to be exhibited,' said Cromartie. 'I'm very grateful to you for having told me the truth about myself.' Then he took off his hat and said 'Good-bye,' and giving a quick little nod he walked away.

'Miserable baboon,' muttered Josephine, and she hurried out through the swing doors.

They were both of them in a rage, but John Cromartie was in such a desperate rage that he did not know he was angry, he only thought that he was very miserable and unhappy. Josephine, on the other hand, was elated. She would have enjoyed slashing at Cromartie with a whip.

That evening Cromartie could not keep still. When the chairs presumed to stand in his path he knocked them over, but he soon found that merely upsetting furniture was not enough to restore his peace of mind. It was then that Mr. Cromartie made a singular determination – one which you may swear no other man in like circumstances would ever have arrived at.

It was somehow or other to get himself exhibited in the Zoo, as if he were part of the menagerie.

It may be that a strange predilection which he had for keeping his word is enough to account for this. But it will always be found that many impulses are entirely whimsical and not to be accounted for by reason. And this man was both proud and obstinate, so that when he had decided upon a thing in passion he would brave it out so far that he could no longer withdraw from it.

At the time he said to himself that he would do it to humiliate Josephine. If she loved him it would make her suffer, and if she did not love him it would not matter to him where he was.

'And perhaps she is right,' he said to himself with a smile.

'Perhaps I am the missing link, and the Zoo is the best place for me.'

He took his pen and a sheet of paper and sat down to write a letter, though he knew that if he achieved his object he would be bound to suffer. For some little while he thought over all the agonies of being in a cage and held up to the derision of the gaping populace.

And then he reflected that it was harder for some of the animals than it would be for himself. The tigers were prouder than he was, they loved their liberty more than he did his, they had no amusements or resources, and the climate did not suit them.

In his case there were no such added difficulties. He told himself that he was humble of heart, and that he resigned his liberty of his own free will. Even if books were not allowed him, he could at all events watch the spectators with as much interest as that with which they watched him.

In this manner he encouraged himself, and the thought of how terrible it was for the tigers touched his heart so much that his own fate seemed to him easier to contemplate.

After all, he reflected, he was so unhappy at that moment that nothing could be worse whatever he did. He had lost Josephine, and it would be easier to bear that loss in the discipline of a prison. Strengthened by these considerations, he shook his pen and wrote as follows: –

Dear Sir,

I write to lay before your Society a proposal which I hope you will recommend to them for their earnest consideration. May I say first that I know the Society's Gardens well, and much admire them? The grounds are spacious, and the arrangement of the houses is at the same time practical and convenient. In them there are specimens of practically the whole fauna of the terrestrial globe, only one mammalian of real importance being unrepresented. But the more I have thought over this omission, the more extraordinary has it appeared to me. To leave out man from a collection of the earth's fauna is to play Hamlet without the Prince of Denmark. It may seem unimportant at first sight, since the collection is formed for man to look at, and study. I admit that human beings are to be seen frequently enough walking about in the Gardens, but I believe that there are convincing reasons why the Society should have a specimen of the human race on exhibition.

Firstly, it would complete the collection, and, secondly, it would impress upon the mind of the visitor a comparison which he is not always quick to make for himself. If placed in a cage between the Orang-outang and the Chimpanzee, an ordinary member of the human race would arrest the attention of everyone who entered the Large Ape-house. In such a position he would lead to a thousand interesting comparisons being made by visitors for whose education the Gardens do in a large measure exist. Every child would grow up imbued with the outlook of a Darwin, and would become aware not only of his own exact place in the animal kingdom, but also in what he resembled, and in what he differed from the Apes. I would suggest that such a specimen be shown as far as possible in his natural surroundings as he exists at the present time, that is to say in ordinary costume, and employed in some ordinary pursuit. Thus his cage should be furnished with chairs and a table and with bookcases. A small bedroom and a bathroom at the back would enable him to retire when necessary from the public gaze. The expense to the Society need not be great.

To show my good faith I beg to offer myself for exhibition, subject to certain reservations which will not be found of an unreasonable nature.

The following particulars of my person may be of assistance: –

Race: Scottish.

Height: 5 feet 11 inches.

Weight: 11 stone.

Hair: Dark.

Eyes: Blue.

Nose: Aquiline.

Age: 27 years.

I shall be happy to furnish any further information which the Society may require.

I am, Sir,

Your obedient Servant,

John Cromartie.

When he had gone out and posted this letter Mr. Cromartie felt at peace, and he prepared for the reply with much less anxiety than most young men would have felt in such a situation.

It would be tedious to describe at any length how this letter was received by a deputy in the absence of the secretary, and how it was by him communicated to the working committee on the following Wednesday. It may, however, be of interest to note that Mr. Cromartie's offer would in all probability have been rejected had it not been for Mr. Wollop. He was a gentleman of advanced years who was not popular with his fellow members. Mr. Cromartie's letter, for some reason, threw him into a paroxysm of rage.

This was a deliberate insult, he declared. This was no laughing matter. It was a matter which must and should and should and must, without question, be wiped out by legal proceedings. It would expose the Society to ridicule if they took it lying down. This and much more in the same strain gave the rest of the committee time to turn the thing over in their minds.

One or two first took the opposite view from Mr. Wollop from mere habit; the Chairman observed that the presence of such an interesting correspondent as Mr. Cromartie could not fail to be a great attraction and would increase the gate-money; it was not, however, until Mr. Wollop threatened to resign that the thing was done.

Mr. Wollop withdrew, and a letter was drafted to Cromartie informing him that the committee were inclined to accept his proposal, and asking for a personal interview.

This interview took place the following Saturday, by which time the committee had become convinced that a specimen of *Homo sapiens* ought certainly to be acquired, though it was not convinced that Mr. Cromartie was the right man, and Mr. Wollop had retired to Wollop Bottom, his rustic seat.

The personal interview was entirely satisfactory to both sides, and Mr. Cromartie's reservations were accepted without demur. These dealt with food and drink, clothing, medical attention, and one or two luxuries which he was to receive. Thus he was to be allowed to order his own meals, see his own tailor, be visited by his own doctor, dentist, and legal advisers. He was to be allowed to administer his own income, which amounted to about £300 a year, neither was objection to be raised to his having a library in his cage, and writing materials.

The Zoological Society on their side stipulated that he should not contribute to the daily or weekly press; that he should not entertain visitors while the Gardens were open to the public; and that he should be subject to the usual discipline, as though he were one of the ordinary creatures.

A few days served to prepare the cage for his reception. It was in the Ape-house, behind which a larger room was furnished for his bedroom, with a bath and lavatory fixed behind a wooden partition. He was admitted on the following Sunday afternoon, and introduced to his keeper Collins, who also looked after the Orang-outang, the Gibbon, and the Chimpanzee.

Collins shook hands and said that he would do all he could to make him comfortable, but it was obvious that he was embarrassed, and strangely enough this embarrassment did not diminish as time went on. His relations with Cromartie always remained formal, and were characterised by the most absolute politeness, which, needless to say, Cromartie scrupulously returned.

The cage had been thoroughly cleansed and disinfected, a plain carpet had been laid down, and it was furnished with a table where Cromartie had his meals, an upright chair, an armchair, and at the back of the cage a bookcase. Nothing but the wire-netting front and sides separating him from the Chimpanzee on one side, and the Orang-outang on the other, distinguished it from a gentleman's study. Greater magnificence characterised the furniture of his bedroom, where he found that he had been provided with every possible comfort. A French bed, a wardrobe, a cheval glass, a dressing-table with mirrors in gilt and satinwood, combined to make him feel at home.

John Cromartie employed Sunday evening in unpacking his

belongings, including his books, as he wished to appear an established institution by the time visitors arrived on the Monday. For this purpose he was given an oil lamp, as the electric wiring had not been completed for the cage.

When he had been busy for a short time he looked about and found something very strange in his situation. In the dimly-lit cage on his right the Chimpanzee moved uneasily; on the other side he could not see the Orang-outang, which must have been hiding in some corner. Outside, the passage was in darkness. He was locked in. At intervals he could hear the cries of different beasts, though he could rarely tell which it was from the cry. Several times he made out the howl of a wolf, and once the roar of a lion. Later the screaming and howling of wild animals became louder and almost incessant.

Long after he had arranged all his books in the shelves and had gone to bed, he lay awake listening to the strange noises. The clamour died away, but he lay waiting for the occasional laugh of the hyaena or the roar of the hippopotamus.

In the morning he was woken early by Collins, who came to ask him what he would have for breakfast and during the day, and added that workmen had come to fix a board at the front of his cage. Cromartie asked if he might see it, and Collins brought it in.

On it was written: –

Homo sapiens

MAN ♂

This specimen, born in Scotland, was presented to the Society by John Cromartie, Esq. Visitors are requested not to irritate the Man by personal remarks.

When Cromartie had had breakfast there was very little to do; he made his bed and began reading 'The Golden Bough.'

Nobody came into the Ape-house until twelve o'clock, when two little girls came in; they looked into his cage, and the younger of them said to her sister:

'What monkey's that? Where is it?'

'I don't know,' said the elder girl. Then she said: 'I believe the man is there to be looked at.'

'Why he's just like Uncle Bernard,' said the little girl.

They looked at Cromartie with an offended stare, and then went on at once to the Orang-outang, who was an old friend. The grown-up people who came in during the afternoon read the notice in a puzzled way, sometimes aloud, and more than once after a hurried glance they went out of the house. They were all embarrassed except a jaunty little man who came in just before closing time. He laughed, and laughed again, and finally he had to sit down on a seat, where he sat choking for three or four minutes, after which he took off his hat to Cromartie and went out of the house saying aloud: 'Splendid! Wonderful! Bravo!'

The next day there were rather more people, but not a great crowd. One or two men came and took photographs, but Mr. Cromartie had already learnt a trick that was to serve him well in his new situation – that of not looking through the bars, so that often he would not know whether there were people watching him or not. Everything was made very comfortable for him, and on that score he was glad enough that he had come.

Yet he could not help asking himself what did his surroundings matter to him? He was in love with Josephine, and now he had parted from her for ever. Would the pain he felt on that account ever die away? And if it did, as he supposed it would, how long would it take to do so?

In the evening he was let out, and walked round the Gardens alone. He tried to make friends with one or two of the creatures, but they would not take notice of him. The evening was cool and fresh, and he was glad to be out of the stuffy Ape-house. He felt it very strange to be alone in the Zoo at that hour, and strange to have to go back to his cage. The next day, just after breakfast, a crowd began pushing into the house, which was soon packed full. The crowd was noisy, some persons in it calling out to him very persistently.

It was easy enough for Cromartie to ignore them, and never let his eyes wander through the wire-netting, but he

could not prevent himself from knowing that they were there. By eleven o'clock his keeper had to fetch four policemen, two standing at each door to keep the crowd back. The people were made to stand in a queue, and to keep moving all the time.

This went on all day, and in fact there were thousands waiting to see 'The Man' who had to be turned away before they could get a sight of him. Collins said it was worse than any bank-holiday.

Cromartie did not betray any uneasiness; he ate his lunch, smoked a cigar, and played several games of Patience, but by tea-time he was exhausted, and would have liked to go and lie down in his bedroom, but it seemed to him that to do so would be to confess weakness. What made it worse, because more ridiculous, was that the Chimpanzee and the Orang-outang next door, each came to the partition walls and spent the whole day staring at him too. No doubt they were only imitating the public in doing so, but they added a great deal to poor Mr. Cromartie's unhappiness. At last the long day was over, the crowds departed, the Gardens were closed, and then came another surprise – for his two neighbours did not go away. No, they clung to the wire partitions and began to chatter and show their teeth at him. Cromartie was too tired to stay in the cage, and went and lay down in his bedroom. When he came back after an hour the Chimpanzee and the

Orang were still there, and greeted him with angry snarls. There was no doubt about it – they were threatening him.

Cromartie did not understand why this should be until Collins, who had come past, explained it to him.

'They are wild with jealousy,' he said, 'that you should have drawn such a large crowd.' And he warned Mr. Cromartie to be very careful not to go within reach of their fingers. They would tear his hair out and kill him if they could get at him.

At first Mr. Cromartie found this very hard to credit, but afterwards, when he got to know the characters of his fellow captives better, it became the most ordinary commonplace. He learnt that all the monkeys, the elephants, and the bears felt jealous in this way. It was natural enough that the creatures that were fed by the public should feel resentment if they were passed over, for they are insatiably greedy, and the worse they digest the food given them the more anxious they are to glut themselves with it. The wolves felt a different jealousy, for they were constantly forming attachments to particular persons among the crowd, and if the chosen person neglected them for a neighbour they became jealous. Only the larger cats, lions, and panthers seemed free from this degrading passion.

During his stay Mr. Cromartie gradually came to know all the beasts in the Gardens pretty well, since he was allowed out every evening after closing-time, and very often was allowed to go into other cages. Nothing struck him more forcibly than the distinction which most of the different creatures very soon drew between him and the keepers. When a keeper came past every animal would pay some attention, whereas few of them would even look round for Mr. Cromartie. He was treated by the vast majority with indifference. As time went on he saw that they treated him as they treated each other, and it struck him that they had somehow learnt that he was being exhibited as they were themselves. This impression was so forcible that Mr. Cromartie believed it without question, though it is not easy to prove that it was so, and still more difficult to explain how such a piece of knowledge could have spread among so heterogeneous a collection of creatures. Yet the attitude of the animals to each other was so marked, that Mr. Cromartie not only observed it in them, but very soon came to feel it in himself for them. He could not describe it better than by calling it firstly 'cynical indifference,' and then adding that it was perfectly good-natured. It was expressed usually by total indifference, but sometimes by something between a yawn of contempt and a grin of cynical appreciation. It was just in these slight shades of manner that Mr. Cromartie found the animals interesting. Naturally they had nothing to say to him, and in such artificial surroundings their natural habits were difficult to ascertain, only those living in families or colonies ever seeming perfectly at their ease, but they all did seem to reveal something of themselves in their attitude to each other. To man they showed quite different behaviour, but in their eyes Mr. Cromartie was not a man. He might smell like one, but they saw at once that he had come out of a cage.

There is in this a possible explanation of the often recorded fact that it is particularly easy for convicts to make friends with mice and rats in prison.

For the rest of that week crowds collected round the new Ape-house every day, and the queue for admittance was longer than that at the pit of Drury Lane Theatre on a first night.

Thousands of people paid for admission to the Gardens and waited patiently for hours in order to catch a glimpse of the new creature which the Society had acquired, and none were really disappointed when they had seen him, although many professed to be so. For everyone went away with what people are most grateful for having – that is, a new subject for conversation, something that everyone could discuss and have an opinion about, viz., the propriety of exhibiting a man. Not that this discussion was confined to those who had actually been successful in catching a glimpse of him. On the contrary it raged in every train, in every drawing room, and in the columns of every newspaper in England. Jokes on the subject were made at public dinners, and at music-halls, and Mr.

17

Cromartie was referred to continually in *Punch*, sometimes in a facetious manner. Sermons were preached about him, and a Labour member in the House of Commons said that when the working classes came into power the rich would be put 'alongside the Man in the Zoo, where they properly belonged.'

What was the strangest thing was that everyone held the view either that a man ought to be exhibited, or that he ought not to be exhibited, and that after a week's time there were not half a dozen men in England who believed no moral principle to be involved in the matter.

Mr. Cromartie cared less than nothing for all these discussions of which he was the subject; it was no more to him indeed what men said about him than if he had been the ape in the cage beside his own. Indeed it was really less, for had the ape been able to understand that thousands of people were talking about it, the creature would have been as much puffed up with pride as now it was mortified with jealousy that its neighbour should draw so vast a crowd.

Mr. Cromartie told himself he cared nothing for the world of men now. As he looked through the meshes of his cage at the excited faces watching him, it cost him an effort to listen to what was being said of him, and after a while his attention wandered even against his will, for he cared nothing for mankind and cared nothing for what they said.

Yet while he told himself that with some complacency, something came into his mind which threw him into such disorder that he looked about him for a minute as if he were distracted, and then ran as if in terror into his hiding-place, his place of refuge, his bedroom, which he had not sheltered in before, at least not in that way.

'What if I should see Josephine among them?' he asked himself aloud, and the thought of her coming was so actual to him that it seemed as if she were at that moment entering the house, and then were there at the bars already.

'What can I do?' he asked himself. 'I can do nothing. What can I say? I can say nothing. No, I must not speak to her, I will not look at her. When I see her I will sit down in my armchair and look on the floor until she is gone, that is, if I have the strength. What will become of me if she should come? And perhaps she will come every day and will be always there watching me through the bars, and will call out and insult me as some do already. How could I bear that?'

Then he asked himself why should she come at all, and began to persuade himself that there was no reason why she should visit him, and that it was the most irrational fear that could seize hold of him – but it would not do.

'No,' said he at length, shaking his head, 'I see she is bound to come. She is free to go where she likes, and one day when I look up I shall see her there, staring into my cage at me. Sooner or later it is bound to happen.' Then he asked himself what errand would send her there to look at him? Why would she come? Would it be to mock at him and torment him, or would it be because now that it was too late she repented of sending him there?

'No,' he told himself, 'no, Josephine will never repent, or if she should, she would not own to it. When she does come here it will be to hurt me more than she has done already; she will come to torture me because it amuses her and I am at her mercy. Oh, God, she has no mercy in her.'

At this Mr. Cromartie who was so proud only a half-hour ago, saying he cared nothing for mankind now and nothing for what they said, began to cry and whimper like a baby, staying hidden all the while in his little bedroom. He sat there on the edge of his bed with his face buried in his hands for a quarter of an hour, and the tears running through his fingers. And all the while he was busy with this new fear of his, and saying to himself first that his life was no longer safe, that Josephine would bring a pistol and shoot him through the bars; and then his thoughts fetching about, that she cared nothing for him, and would not come to hurt him, but from mere love of notoriety and to get herself talked about by her friends or in the newspapers. At last he pulled himself somewhat together, washed his face and bathed his eyes, and then went back into his cage, where you may be sure the crowd was pretty impatient to see him after being kept waiting so long.

Once again you could see how this Mr. Cromartie 'cared nothing for mankind and what they said.' For the moment that he stepped into his cage in full view of the public, from being an abject creature with his face comically twisted up to keep back his tears, he became at once quite calm and self-possessed and showed no trace of any feeling. Yet did this assumed calm show that he cared nothing for mankind? Was it because he cared nothing for mankind that he made these efforts, swallowing down the lump that was risen in his throat, holding back the tear that would have started to his eye, and strolling in with a serene smile, then knitting his brows with an affectation of thought; and was all this because he cared nothing for mankind?

The strange thing was that Mr. Cromartie should have taken three weeks to think that Josephine would certainly come and pay him a visit. For three weeks he had been thinking at every moment of the day of this girl Josephine, and, indeed, dreaming of her almost every night, but it had never come into his head that he would ever see her again. He had told himself a thousand times, 'We are parted for ever,' and had never asked himself, 'Why do I say this?' He had, one evening, even retraced their steps as they had wandered from one cage to another on the day that they had had their final rupture. But now all these sentimental ideas were a thousand miles away from him, who, though he lay back, yawned, and negligently cut the pages of a book from Mudie's, was all the same terrified at the question he kept asking himself:

'When will she come? Will she come now, to-day, or perhaps to-morrow? Will she not come till next week, or not for a month?'

And his heart shrank within him as he understood that he would never know when she was coming and he would never be prepared for her.

But with all this flutter Mr. Cromartie was like a countryman coming into town a day late for the fair, for

Josephine had already paid him a visit that day two hours before he had ever thought that she might do so.

When she had come Josephine did not know at all certainly why she found herself there. Every day since she had heard of the 'loathsome thing' John had done she had vowed that she would never see him again, and would never think of him again. Every day she spent in thinking of him, and every day her anger drove her to walk in the direction of Regent's Park, and all her time was occupied in thinking how she could best punish him for what he had done.

At first it had been insupportable for her. She had heard the news from her father at breakfast while he was reading *The Times*, and had learnt it in fragments as he chanced to read it out to her while she sat silent with the coffee machine and the egg machine in front of her, for her father stickled for his eggs being boiled very exactly. When breakfast was over she found *The Times* and read the account of the 'Startling Acquisition by the Zoo Authorities.' She told herself then that she could never forgive or forget the insult to which she had been subjected, and that while she sat at breakfast she had grown an old woman.

As time went on Josephine's fury did not slacken; no, it became greater; and it passed through a dozen or more phases every day. Thus at one moment she would laugh with pity for such a poor fool as John, in the next marvel that such a creature should have the sense to know where he belonged, then turn all her rage on the Zoological Society for causing such an outrage to decency to occur their grounds, and reflect bitterly on the folly of mankind who were ready to divert themselves at such a sorry spectacle as the degraded John – reducing themselves indeed to his level. Again, she would exclaim at the vanity which led him to such a course; anything would do so long as he got himself talked about. No doubt he would see that she, Josephine, was talked about too. Indeed, John, she declared, had done it solely to affront her. But he had gone the wrong way to work if he thought he would impress her. She would indeed go to see him and show him how little she cared for him; no, what was better, she would go visit the other ape next door to him. That was the way by which she could best show him her indifference to him, and her superiority to the vulgar mob of sightseers. Nothing would induce her to look at such a base creature as John. She could not regard his action with indifference. It was a calculated insult, but fortunately he would alone suffer for it, for as for herself she had never cared in the least for him, and her complete indifference was not likely to be ruffled by his latest escapade. Indeed it meant no more to her than any other creature being exhibited.

Thus Miss Lackett drove round and round in circles, vowing vengeance at one time and the next moment swearing that it was all one to her what he did, she had never cared for him and never would. But do what she might she could think of nothing else. At night she lay awake saying to herself first one thing and then another, and changing her mind ten times for every time she turned her head on the pillow, and thus she spent the first three or four days and nights in misery.

Yet in all this there was something that wounded Miss Lackett more even than the fact itself, and that was the consciousness of her own worthlessness and vulgarity. Everything she felt, everything she said, was vulgar. Her preoccupation with Mr. Cromartie was vulgar, and every emotion connected with him which she now felt was degrading. In fact, after the first few days this weighed on her so heavily that she was almost ready to forgive him, but she could never forgive herself. All her self-respect was gone for ever, she told herself; henceforward she knew that she was never disinterested. She had offended herself more than any number of Cromarties would ever do. She was, she said, deeply disappointed in herself, and wondered how it had come about that this side of her nature should have been so long unsuspected by her.

It was this turning off of her rage and indignation against herself that finally allowed of her going to see him, or rather of her going to see the Chimpanzee next to him, for she repeated to herself that she would not look at him, that she could not endure to see him, and so on, though at moments this decision was modified by the reflection that she only hoped he would feel properly punished when he saw her give him one glance of cool contempt.

Miss Lackett found the event different from her expectations. In front of the Ape-house a crowd was collected, and directly she had joined it she found herself caught up in a queue of people waiting to see 'The Man.' On all sides she heard jokes about him, and those of the women (who were in the majority) struck her as being barely decent. Progress was extremely slow and very exhausting.

At last, when she found herself in the building itself, it was impossible for her to carry out her intention of looking only at the apes, for she suddenly became overcome at the thought of seeing them and closed her eyes lest she should see an ape and be overcome by nausea. In a few minutes she found herself in front of Cromartie's cage, and gazed at him helplessly. At that moment he was engaged in walking up and down (which occupation, by the way, took up far more of his time than he ever suspected). But she could not speak to him, indeed she dreaded that he should see her.

Back and forth he walked by the wire division, with his hands behind his back and his head bent slightly, until he reached the corner, when up went his head and he turned on his heel. His face was expressionless.

Before she got out Miss Lackett was to have another shock, for, leaving Mr. Cromartie's cage, she let her eyes wander and suddenly was looking straight into the mug of the Orang. This creature sat disconsolately on the floor with her long red hair matted and entangled with straws. Her close-set brown eyes were staring in front of her and nothing about her moved but her black nostrils, that were the shape of an inverted heart and set in a mask of black and dusty rubber. This, then, was the creature that her lover resembled! It was to this melancholy Caliban that everyone compared him! Such a hideous monster as this ape was thought a suitable companion for the man with whom she had imagined herself in love! For the man whom she had considered marrying!

Miss Lackett slipped silently out of the house, sick with

disgust and weighed down with shame. She was ashamed of everything, of her own feelings, of her weakness in caring what happened to John. She was ashamed of the spectators, of herself, and of the dirty world where such men, and beasts like them, existed. Mixed with her shame was fear which grew greater with every step she took. She was alarmed lest she would be recognised, and looked at everyone she passed with nervous apprehension; even after she had got out of the Gardens she did not feel safe, so that she got herself a taxi and climbed in almost breathlessly, and even then looked behind her through the pane of glass in the back. Nothing followed her.

'Thank God, it is all right. There is no danger,' she said to herself, though what the danger was of which she spoke she could not have said. Perhaps she was afraid that she might be shut up in a cage herself.

The next day Miss Lackett had somewhat shaken off the painful impressions caused by her visit, and her chief emotion was a sensible relief that it had turned out no worse.

'Never again,' she said to herself, 'shall I be guilty of such folly. Never again,' she repeated, 'need I run such an awful risk. Never again shall I think of that poor fellow, for I shall never need to. Out of justice to him I had to see him, even though at a distance, and without his seeing me. It would have been cowardly not to have gone, it would not have been in keeping with my character. But it would be cowardice in me to go again. It would be weak. After all I had to indulge my curiosity, it would have been fatal to have suppressed it. Now I know the worst and the affair is closed for ever. If I were to go again it would be painful to me and unjust to him, for I might be recognised; if he heard that I had been twice it would fill him with false hopes. He might conclude that I wished to speak with him. Nothing, nothing could be farther from the truth. I think he is mad. I feel sure he is mad. Talking to him would be like those interviews that people have to have once a year with their insane relatives. But fortunately for me my duty coincides with my inclinations – I ought not to see him and I abhor the thought of doing so. There is no more to be said.'

It was not often that Miss Lackett was so consistent in her thoughts, neither, we may add, was she often quite so prim. She managed to repeat such phrases over and over again to herself throughout the week, but somehow she did not succeed in forgetting all about Mr. Cromartie, or even in putting him out of her thoughts for more than an hour or two at a time.

On the fourth day after her visit it so happened that General Lackett gave a dinner-party at which his daughter acted as hostess. Several of the guests were young, and one or two of them not very well-to-do. It was natural in these circumstances, as the General had rather thoughtlessly dismissed his chauffeur for the evening, that his daughter should offer to drive some of her young friends home. One of them lived in Frognal, two others in Circus Road, St. John's Wood. On the outward journey Miss Lackett took the ordinary route from Eaton Square, that is, by Park Lane, Baker Street, Lord's, and the Finchley Road as far as Frognal, afterwards bringing her other companions back to Circus Road.

It was then, after saying good-bye, and good-bye again as she drove away, that she gave way to a feeling of unrest. She drove slowly to Baker Street station, but by that time she was thinking of Mr. Cromartie. This caused her, almost mechanically, to swing her car round to the left, and shortly afterwards to take the Outer Circle. As she drove, her mind was almost blank; she was driving in that direction merely to dissipate a mood. All she was conscious of was that Cromartie was there – in the Zoo. She was tired, and driving distracted her. In a few moments she was passing the Gardens. She pulled up just over the tunnel, before reaching the main entrance. At this point she was as close as she could get to the new Ape-house, which lay, as she knew, under the shadow of the Mappin Terraces. She got out of the car and walked up to the palings. They were too high for her to look over, and when she pulled herself up by her hands there was nothing to be seen but the black shadows of evergreens and, through one break in them, a corner of the Mappin Terraces – a silhouette of black against the moonlight. As she looked it came into her head that it was like something familiar to her. Her wrists ached and she jumped down.

'John, John, why are you in there?' she said aloud. In a few moments she saw a policeman approaching her, so she got back into her car and drove on slowly.

As she passed the main entrance she turned again, and again she saw the Mappin Terraces.

'The Tower of Babel, of course,' she said aloud, 'in Chambers's Encyclopedia. It's like Noah's Ark, too, I suppose, as it's a menagerie, and – Oh, curse! Oh, damn!' There were tears in her eyes, and the street lamps had become little circular rainbows. But what she said to herself was that it was awkward driving.

That night she could not sleep, and could find none of the ordinary defences against unhappiness. That is to say, she was unable to affect any kind of superiority to her troubles, besides which she saw them exactly as they were, in their naked horror, and was not able to put them in conventional categories. For could Miss Lackett have said to herself: 'I have been in love with John, now I find he is mad. This is a terrible tragedy, it is very painful to think of people being mad, for me it is a disappointment in love. Such disappointments are the most painful to which a girl in my position can be exposed,' and so on – if she could have done this then Miss Lackett would have found a sure way to reduce her suffering to a minimum. For by putting forward such general ideas as madness and disappointment in love she could very soon have come to feel only the general emotion suited to these ideas. But as it was she could only think of John Cromartie, his face, voice, manners, and way of moving; of the particular cage in which she had last seen him, the smell of apes, the swarm of people staring at him and laughing, and of her own loneliness and misery which John had deliberately caused. That is to say she thought only of her pain, and did not cast about to give it a name. And naming a sorrow is a first step to forgetting it. About three o'clock in the morning she got out of bed and went down to the dining room, where she found a decanter of port, another of whisky, and some Bath Olivers. She poured herself out a glass of port and tasted it, but its sweetness disgusted her, so she put it down and helped herself to the whisky. After she had got down half a wineglass of the spirit, taking it neat as it came from the bottle, she felt much calmer. She drank another glass of it and then went up to her room, threw herself on her bed, and at once fell into a heavy, drunken sleep.

During these days Mr. Cromartie had by no means got rid of his apprehensions of seeing Josephine. The thought which tormented him most was that he was at her mercy, that is to say, that she was at liberty to visit him whenever she liked, and to stay away as long as she chose. The material conditions of his life did not change in any degree, though there was no longer a vast crowd anxious to see him at all times; and from four policemen, two were soon thought to be enough to regulate his visitors. After another week the two were reduced to one, but though the crowd was scantier each day this policeman was left permanently, more as a protection for Mr. Cromartie than anything else, for certain persons had shown themselves very disobliging to him. Indeed, Mr. Cromartie had had to complain on two occasions, and that not only of abusive language. But during this time very little had changed in his material surroundings; this is not saying there was no alteration in Mr. Cromartie's state of mind. In that respect there were two forces at work. One was that he was now continually thinking of Josephine and expecting a visit from her, and, that as his circle of ideas grew smaller in solitude, he became more and more taken up by imagining how she would come, what she would say, and so forth. Thus he was continually rehearsing scenes with Josephine, and this habit interfered with his daily reading and at times even alarmed him about his sanity. In the second place, perhaps because thinking so much of Josephine made him withdraw into himself, he became shy, was annoyed by the spectators, and felt something approaching a repulsion for the animals in the menagerie.

This feeling was naturally intensified in regard to his immediate neighbours, the female Orang and the Chimpanzee. In their case he was indeed only making a slight return for the ill will they bore him, which seemed to increase with every day. Mr. Cromartie was really much to blame for an aggravation of their natural and, one may say, reasonable dislike of him. For not only did he draw a larger crowd than fell to their share, but he persistently ignored them, and so neglected ordinary civilities that he would have made himself exceedingly unpopular had his neighbours been human beings like himself. This was due to a singular defect of imagination in him rather than to natural want of manners, for in ordinary life he always showed himself perfectly well bred. If an excuse can be found for his conduct it is that he believed that the proper thing for him to do was to ignore the very existence of his neighbours, and also that Collins, his keeper, never set him right on this point. The fact is that Collins was never perfectly easy with Mr. Cromartie, and that he was the kind of man to take offence himself. Indeed, he was more jealous of the feelings of his old favourites, the two apes, than he was quite aware of. Besides this he had lost the Gibbon, which had been given to another keeper when Mr. Cromartie had come, and there is no hiding the fact that Collins would have liked to have the Gibbon back in Mr. Cromartie's place. For one thing the ape had given him less work, and for another, it had never been at any time in its life his social superior. Besides that, Collins had, for we should do him justice, a very positive affection for the animal. One evening, after a day passed in a most desultory way, Mr. Cromartie was sitting in his cage sucking his pipe, when suddenly he saw Miss Lackett come into the empty house.

This was the evening of the day after her troubled night. In the morning she had resolved to settle the question whether Cromartie were mad or not, to make a judgment on the subject that would be impartial and definitive, for she felt convinced that if she could not settle the question of his sanity one way or the other, there would be no doubt of her losing hers.

But when she had got into the Gardens she found it impossible to see Mr. Cromartie alone. A crowd, though not as large as formerly, was still clustered round the Ape-house the whole of the morning. Between one and two there were always some persons before his cage whose presence rendered it impossible for her to speak with him. She saw then that the only thing was for her to wait till last thing at night and to hurry in just at closing time. All this delay upset the arrangements of her day. The knowledge that she had promised to call for her old schoolfellow, Lady Rebecca Joel, and to go on and take tea at Admiral Goshawk's, and to go out afterwards with them, worried her excessively. At the last minute she sent messages pleading headache and indisposition, and then found nothing to do until closing time at the Zoo. To stay in the Gardens for so long was intolerable. To add to her discomfort the sky clouded over and a sharp storm came on, the air soon being filled with sleet, snowflakes and hailstones. She ran out of the Gardens, getting wet as she did so, and it was some moments before she could find a taxi. When once inside there was the absolute necessity of telling the man where to take her.

'Baker Street,' said she. For Baker Street is a central point from which she could easily go wherever she wished. This was the reason, it will be remembered, that made the great detective Holmes choose to have his rooms in Baker Street, and to-day it is still more central. All Metro-Land is at one's feet.

But the time taken between the Zoo and Baker Street Tube station is short, and Miss Lackett arrived with no clearer idea of where to go or what to do than she had when she first ran out of the Gardens. To be sure the rain had stopped for the time being, and she walked briskly along the Marylebone Road. For she belonged to the order of society which cannot loiter in the street. She marched away without any purpose, wondering what she would do with herself, when on came the storm again with a sudden gush of rain. Josephine looked about her and found a refuge offered by the gates of a large red-brick building, which she entered. It was Madame Tussaud's.

She had never as a child visited the celebrated collection of wax-work effigies, and she was at once interested in what she saw there. Some internal voice bade her make the most of this casual opportunity, to throw aside her temporary unhappiness, and enjoy herself.

She fell into a peaceful state of mind, and for several hours in succession gave herself up to the pleasure of gazing at the formal figures of the most celebrated persons of this and former ages. For the most part they were the great Victorians and dated from last century. There were but few other visitors, but the great saloons are always crowded, and everywhere that she looked she found familiar faces.

Josephine had been presented at Court, but had not been impressed by the experience. Madame Tussaud's seemed to her like a more august presentation at an Eternal Levee.

At one end of the room there were indeed the royal families of Europe in their coronation robes. There was an air of formality, a stiffness, and a constraint in all present which seemed to her natural in guests waiting for their host to come in. And perhaps in another moment a curtain would be brushed aside, and the Host of Hosts would appear.

Josephine did not wait any longer, but ran downstairs to the Chamber of Horrors.

Before it seemed possible it was time to go back to the Gardens, if she were to see Cromartie before closing time. She walked quickly into the house, and found Cromartie sitting near the front of his cage as if he were expecting to see her. As she came up to the cage he put down the pipe he had been holding in his mouth and stood up, seeming then to overshadow her, the floor of his cage being higher than the corridor in which she stood.

'Please sit down,' she said, and then was silent, finding nothing of all the things she had come to tell him ready to her tongue.

He obeyed her.

They looked then at each other for some little while in

silence. At last Josephine summoned up her resolution and said to him, speaking in a low voice:

'I think that you are mad.'

Cromartie nodded his head; he had huddled himself up in his chair and apparently was unable to speak.

Josephine waited and said: 'I was very worried about you, because I thought at first that something I had said to you might have made you behave in this idiotic way, but it is now quite clear to me that even if what I said did have any influence, you are quite mad, and that I need not think about you any more.'

Cromartie nodded his head again. She noticed with some surprise that he was weeping, and that his face was wet with tears which were falling on to the floor of his cage. The sight of his tears and his determined silence made her harden her heart. She felt suddenly angry.

The bell began ringing for closing time, and she heard someone, probably the policeman, with his hand on the door talking to another man outside. Josephine turned away, but a moment afterwards came back to the cage. Cromartie was walking away from her blowing his nose.

'You must be mad,' she called after him; then the door opened and the policeman came in.

'Hurry up, Miss, or you'll have to stay here all night, and you know that would never do,' she heard him say as she hurried away.

Though Josephine's visit had been painful, it did not succeed in distressing Cromartie for very long. Indeed, after a short time he recovered himself completely, and reasoning upon what she had said, and the reasons of her coming at all, he found much with which to comfort himself. In the first place, all the secret doubts he had had in the last week of his own sanity were now dissipated. He was not going to believe that he was mad, he said to himself, simply because Josephine Lackett told him so. Besides which, he felt sure that she only affirmed that he was mad because it suited her to believe it. If he were actually insane it would relieve her of any necessity of thinking of him, and that she had felt any such necessity to exist was in itself extremely gratifying. Furthermore, he felt certain that if Josephine had really been convinced of his insanity she would not have paid him a visit in order to tell him of it. Even Josephine would not find any satisfaction in such useless inhumanity. If she felt bound to take any steps in the matter she would have gone to the officers of the Society and insisted that he should be examined by a mental doctor, and if necessary certified as a lunatic. And with these very satisfactory reasons Mr. Cromartie assured himself that he was not really mad, or even in any danger of becoming so, though he did not doubt that Josephine would readily persuade herself to the contrary.

Happiness and misery are purely relative, and Mr. Cromartie was now raised into a state of the highest spirits by considerations which would not ordinarily produce such a result. But after the condition of complete despair in which he had been plunged for several weeks, he could hardly imagine any greater bliss than knowing that Josephine was having to persuade herself that he was mad in order to be able to dismiss him from her thoughts.

But it must not be concluded from this that Mr. Cromartie indulged in any sort of hope. He did not even consider the possibility of escaping from the Zoo or of winning Josephine's love, because he had never had any ambition to do either. Such thoughts would have seemed to him not only ridiculous but also dishonourable. He had taken his course with his eyes open, and the question whether he should abide by it or not was not even open to consideration. In this respect the Zoological Society were indeed fortunate in their selection of a man. For though there is little doubt that Mr. Cromartie would have been given his liberty whenever he asked for it, without his having recourse to extreme measures such as refusing food or imploring the aid of visitors in rescuing him, yet letting him go would have been a cause of vexation to the Society. It is not to be supposed that there would have been any difficulty in replacing him by another specimen of his species. No, the reason why they would have felt his loss such a severe blow is because the public readily attaches itself to the individual animals in the Zoo, and is not to be consoled when such a favourite dies, or disappears, even if it is instantly replaced by an even finer specimen of the same species. Many persons habitually resort to the Gardens in order to visit their particular friends, Sam, Sadie and Rollo, and not merely to look at any polar bear, orang, or king penguin. And this applies quite as forcibly to the Fellows of the Society as to the outside public. It was natural, therefore, that they should entertain hopes that the new acquisition to the Gardens should remain in it for the rest of his natural life, and though he could not vie with the other creatures in general popularity when once the vulgar curiosity about him had worn off, yet it was to be hoped that in time he would develop as much personality as if he were a bear or an ape.

While Sir James Agate-Agar was being shown over the house by the curator, he referred to Cromartie as 'your local Diogenes.' The name was immediately on the lips of everyone who moved in Zoological circles. There was opportunity here for Mr. Cromartie had he been disposed to take it. When once the vulgar publicity which had attended his installation had passed, there were many persons in the upper ranks of London society who were anxious to make Mr. Cromartie's acquaintance, and had he known enough to take up the part marked out for him, there is no doubt but that he could have had as much society as he cared for, and that of persons of the very front rank, all of whom were animated by the most genuine interest in him and friendliness towards him, though naturally not without the expectation that they would in exchange be entertained by his remarks, for such a man as the Diogenes of the Zoo must surely be a great oddity.

But though Mr. Cromartie had every intention of remaining for the rest of his life in the cage provided for him, he had no idea of the social opportunities which doing so would afford him, and he appreciated them so little that he most steadily repulsed all overtures of the kind, and betrayed an obvious reluctance to enter into conversation with anyone, even the curator himself. At the time in question, however, this was set down to a not unnatural self-consciousness in the new situation in which he found himself, and also to the disturbing effect of being exhibited daily to a large crowd, among whom there were persons whose offensive behaviour excited the greatest indignation.

It was several days after this first interview before he was to see Miss Lackett again. During this period he had much to think of, but his spirits remained high; for the first time for ten days he took a walk round the Gardens from pleasure, and not from a feeling that he must have some fresh air if he were to keep well. For several evenings he sat motionless for half an hour or more near the beavers' and the otters' pools, and was frequently rewarded by a glimpse of the former, though only on one occasion by the latter. Whatever creatures in the Gardens had most retained their native wildness were sure to attract him. They seemed to him, in his rather warped state of mind, to have preserved their self-respect. It was to accomplish this in his own particular case which was his chief concern, though of course he was perfectly well aware that it did not consist in behaving with any shyness. On the contrary, Mr. Cromartie's self-respect depended upon his maintaining an appearance of unruffled calm, together with the utmost civility in all his relations with those with whom he had any business.

One evening as he was watching for the foxes, the keeper of the small cats' house came up to him and entered into conversation. After a few trivial remarks which served their ordinary purpose – that is they let Mr. Cromartie know that the keeper was a pleasant fellow and well-disposed to him – he said:

'I think it would be a good plan if you were to make a pet of one of the animals, that is, if you would like to. It seems a waste for you to be here and not make one of the out-of-way kind of pets.'

Mr. Cromartie had been thinking that day that perhaps the greatest disadvantage under which he lay in his situation, was that he could not have any familiar friend. His former life had been utterly renounced and was now closed to him, so that it was no use his looking backwards for one. At the same time he was so utterly cut off from the ordinary run of humanity that he would not care to risk having any intercourse with his fellows lest he should be exposed to pity, or to an offensive curiosity.

The suggestion of this keeper could not have come at a better time, for he saw that though he might not care for a *pet* he might make a *friend*. In any case, he reflected, equality of circumstances is an excellent basis for any acquaintanceship, and he could nowhere share the circumstances of an animal's life so well as he could here in the Zoo. Had he gone into a tropical jungle it would have been no closer, for there, though the animals would have been at home, he would not.

He followed the keeper into the small cat house, and talked with him for a little while longer.

It so happened that one of the beasts directly under the care of this man had attracted Mr. Cromartie when he went into the house before. For in the Caracal he saw an unhappiness to match his own, combined with beauty. The Caracal, poor creature, never stopped moving, holding its face to the bars of its little cage. It moved back and forth with tireless rapidity, and a monotony which seemed inspired by unutterable sorrow.

At his request the keeper now took out the Caracal for him to speak to it.

For several days after this Mr. Cromartie never failed to pay the Caracal a visit every evening, and while making very few overtures to it, he showed the creature that he was more disposed to be friendly than most of its fellow captives. This persistence was not thrown away, for after five or six days the Caracal would stop his sad motions before his bars when Cromartie came in, and would look after him with evident regret when the time came for him to go away.

The keeper, on his side, was mightily pleased at his Caracal's getting such a companion, and perhaps the more so as it was not his own favourite; in particular the man gave himself all the credit for advising Mr. Cromartie to make a pet of some beast or other. It was not long before he spread

the news of it, telling the curator and others of the staff who
might be interested.

The upshot of all this was that one evening as Cromartie
was sitting reading, locked in for the night, suddenly he heard
the door unlocked and beheld the curator come to pay him a
visit.

'Oh, I just stepped in, Mr. Cromartie,' said the curator in
the most friendly way, 'for a word or two. The keeper of the
small cats' house tells me that you have made quite a pet of
the Caracal.'

At these words Cromartie turned a little pale, and said to
himself: 'The fat is in the fire now. He is going to forbid us
continuing our friendship; I ought to have expected it.'

The next words the curator said quite undeceived him, for
he went on: 'Now how would you like, Mr. Cromartie, to
have that fellow in your – in with you here, I mean? You need
not have him unless you like, of course, and you need not
keep him a day longer than you want to. I am not trying to
save space, I assure you.'

Mr. Cromartie accepted the suggestion thankfully, and it
was agreed that the Caracal should come and pay him a trial
visit for a few days.

The next evening he went as usual to the small cat house,
but this time when the Caracal was let out he invited him to
come back with him, and with very little demur the creature
followed him and then walked with him by his side, and then,
his confidence increasing, the cat ran before him a few yards,
stopping every now and then as if to ask him:

'Which way shall we go now, comrade?'

Then as Cromartie came up with him he shook the tassels
of his tufted ears and again ran on before. You may be sure
that the poor Caracal did not suffer from nostalgia for his
little cage. No, indeed, he ran into his friend's more
commodious quarters as if he would be content to stay in
them for ever, and after he had trotted all round them four or
five times and leapt up on to the table and down off each of
the chairs, he settled down as if he were at home, and perhaps

indeed he was so for the first time since he was come to the Gardens.

This pretty kind of cat, for such he found the Caracal to be (not but what it had some virtues for which cats are not usually famous), proved a very great solace to him in his captivity. For the creature had a thousand playful tricks and pretty ways which were a delight to him. For so long he had not been able to see anything all day except his neighbours the sordid apes, and the staring faces of a crowd which seemed to share all the qualities of those apes (and with less excuse for being there), that it was a rare kind of happiness for him to have a graceful and charming creature beside him. Moreover it was his companion, the friend of his choice, and the sharer of his misfortunes. They were equals in everything, and there was in their love none of that fawning servility on the one side and domineering ownership on the other that makes nearly all the dealings of men and animals so degrading to each of the parties. Though it may seem fanciful, there was actually a strong resemblance in the characters of these two friends.

Both were in their nature gay and sportive, with pleasant manners which admirably concealed the untamed wildness of their tawny hearts. But the resemblance lay chiefly in their excessive and stubborn pride. In both of them pride was the mainspring of all their actions, though necessarily the quality must show itself very differently in a man and in a rare and precious kind of a cat. In imprisonment, though in one case it was voluntarily made, and in the other case forced, neither would fawn or make utter and complete submission.

For though Mr. Cromartie always showed a complete resignation and exemplary obedience, yet it was only a feigned submission after all.

The visit of his new friend was to the liking of both parties, and in general they found none of the difficulties that sometimes attend living at close quarters. It is true that the Caracal was no sleeper at night, but spent all the early part of it prowling hither and thither; still it was on very silent and padded feet, and by morning he would be tired of roaming, so that on waking up Mr. Cromartie never failed to find his friend curled up on the bed beside him.

In all their relations the man never attempted to exercise any authority over the beast; if the Caracal wandered away he did not call him back, nor did he try to tempt him with any tit-bits from his table, nor by rewards of any sort train him to new tricks. Indeed, to look at them both together it would seem as if they were unaware of each other's presence, or that nothing but a total indifference existed between them. Only if the Caracal trespassed too far on his patience, either by eating his food before he had finished, or by playing with his pen if he were writing, would he swear at him or give him a little cuff to show his displeasure. Once or twice on such occasions the Caracal bared his teeth at him and stretched out his sharp and wicked claws, but yet he always thought again before using them on his big, slowly moving friend. Once or twice, of course, as might have been expected, Mr. Cromartie got scratched, but this was done in play or was merely accidental; indeed, it almost always was when the Caracal, leaping up from the ground upon his shoulder, held on lest he should over-balance. Only once was this at all serious, and then because the Caracal, trying a higher jump than usual, landed on his head and the nape of his neck. Mr. Cromartie cried out in surprise and pain, and the Caracal drew in his claws instantly, and by purring and many affectionate rubbings of his body against his friend, sought to make amends for his misdeed. Mr. Cromartie was bleeding from ten dagger wounds on his scalp, but after the first moment he spoke gently to the cat and forgave him fully. All this was, however, nothing when weighed against the happiness he had in having a companion to be with him in his captivity, and a companion who was so much the happier for having him.

At Cromartie's request the Caracal was now installed permanently with him, and another board was attached to the front of the cage, beside his own. It bore the inscription:

CARACAL

Felis Caracal. ♂ Iraq.

Presented by Squadron N, R.A.F., Basra.

There were no pictures attached of either Man or Caracal, as it was taken for granted that visitors would be able to distinguish them. The public showed a great appreciation of the Man's sharing his cage with an animal, and Mr. Cromartie suddenly became, what he had not been before, extremely popular. The tide turned, and everybody found charming the person who had so scandalised them. Instead of ill-natured remarks, or even insults, Mr. Cromartie's ears were assailed with cries of delight.

This change was certainly one for the better, though Mr. Cromartie reflected that in time it might become as tedious as ill-natured remarks had been formerly. His defence was the same against each, that is, he shut his ears, never looked through the netting if he could help it, and read his books as if he were indeed a scholar working in his own study.

He was sitting in this way reading 'Wilhelm Meister,' with his companion the Caracal at his feet, when he suddenly heard his name called and looked up.

There was Josephine, standing before him, looking in at him, her face pale, her mouth rigid, and her eyes staring.

Up jumped Mr. Cromartie, but as he was surprised his self-control was gone for an instant.

'My God! What have you come for?' he asked her in agitated tones.

Josephine was taken aback for a moment by this greeting, and as he strode to the front of his cage, stepped back away from him. For the moment she was confused. Then she said:

'I have come to ask you about a book. The second volume of "Les Liaisons Dangereuses." Aunt Eiley is fussing about it. She says the plates make it a very valuable edition. She suspects me of reading it too, and thinks it unsuitable . . .'

As she spoke Cromartie began laughing, screwing up his eyes and showing his teeth.

'So my forgetfulness has got you into a scrape, has it?' he asked. Then: 'I'm most awfully sorry. I've actually got it here. I'll post it to you to-night. I can't slip it through the wire netting, unfortunately. That's one of the drawbacks of living in a cage.'

Josephine had not seen Cromartie looking so charming for a long time. Her own expression changed also, but she still remained shy and awkward, and was obviously afraid of someone coming into the Ape-house and finding them together, talking.

For a moment or two they were silent. She looked at the Caracal and said:

'I read in the paper about your having a companion. I expect it is a very good plan. You are looking better. I've been having bronchitis, and have been laid up for a fortnight since you saw me last.'

But as Josephine spoke Cromartie's face clouded over again. He noticed her awkwardness and was annoyed by it. He remembered also her last visit, and how she had behaved then. Recollecting all this he frowned, drew himself up, rubbed his nose rather crossly, and said:

'You must realise, Josephine, that seeing you is excessively painful to me. In fact I am not sure I can endure being exposed to the danger of it any longer. Last time you came to see me for the purpose of informing me that you think I am mad. I don't think you are right, but if I cannot guard myself from seeing you I daresay I shall go mad. I must therefore ask you in the interests of my own health, if for nothing else, never to come near me again. If you have anything to say of an urgent nature – if there should be another book of yours, or any reason of that sort, you can always write to me. Nothing you can say or do can be anything but extremely painful and exhausting, even if you felt kindly disposed towards me; but from your behaviour I can only conclude you want to give me pain and come here to amuse yourself by hurting me. I warn you I am not going to submit to being tortured.'

'I've never heard such nonsense, John. I hoped you were better, but now I am sure you really are mad,' said Josephine. 'I've never been spoken to in such a way. And you imagine that I of all people want to see you!'

'Well, I forbid your coming to see me in the future,' said Mr. Cromartie.

'Forbid! You forbid!' cried Josephine, who was now furious with him. 'You forbid me to come! Don't you realise that you are being exhibited? I, or anyone else who pays a shilling, can come and stare at you all day. Your feelings need not worry us; you should have thought of that before. You wanted to make an exhibition of yourself, now you must take the consequences. Forbid me to come and look at you! Good heavens! The impertinence of the animal! You are one of the apes now, didn't you know that? You put yourself on a level with a monkey and you are a monkey, and I for one am going to treat you like a monkey.'

This was said in a cold, sneering sort of way that was altogether too much for Mr. Cromartie. The blood flew to his head, and with a face distorted with almost insane rage he shook his fist at her through the bars. When at last he was able to speak it was only to tell her in an unnatural voice:

'I shall kill you for that. Confound these bars!'

'They have some advantages,' said Josephine coolly. She was frightened, but as she spoke Mr. Cromartie lay down on the floor of his cage and she saw him stuff his handkerchief

41

into his mouth and bite it; there were tears in his eyes, and sometimes he fetched a deep groan as if he were near his end.

All this frightened Josephine more even than his threatening that he would murder her. And seeing him rolling there as if he were in a fit made her repent of what she had said to him, and then she came right up to the netting of his cage and began to beg him to forgive her, and to forget what she had said.

'I did not mean one word of it, dearest John,' said she in a new and altered voice, which scarce reached to him, it was so soft. ' How can you think I want to hurt you when I come to this wretched prison of yours to see you because I love you, and cannot forget you in spite of all that you have done only on purpose to hurt me?'

'Oh, go away, go away, if you have any pity left in you,' said John. His own voice was now come back to him, but he sobbed once or twice between his words.

Meanwhile the Caracal, who had watched all this scene and listened to it with a great deal of wonder, now came up to him and began to comfort him in his distress, first sniffing at his face and hands and then licking them.

And before anything more could be said between Josephine and John, the door opened and a whole party of people were come in to see the apes. At that Josephine went out of the house and out of the Gardens, and getting into a cab went straight home, all as if she were in a nightmare. As for Mr. Cromartie, he struggled quickly on to his feet and hurried out of his cage into his hiding-place to wash his face, comb his hair, and compose himself a little before facing the public; but when he went back the party were gone away and there was only his Caracal staring at him and asking him as plain as words:

'What is the matter, my dear friend? Are you all right now? Is it over? I am sorry for you, although I am a Caracal and you are a man. Indeed, I do love you very tenderly.'

There was only the Caracal when he went back into his cage, only the Caracal and 'Wilhelm Meister' lying on the floor.

That night Miss Lackett suffered every torment which love can give, for her pride seemed to have deserted her now when she most wanted it to support her, and without it her pity for poor Mr. Cromartie and her shame at her own words were free to reduce and humble her utterly.

'How can I ever speak to him again?' she asked herself. 'How can I ever hope to be forgiven when I have gone twice to him in his miserable captivity, and each time I have insulted him and said the things which it would hurt him most to hear?'

'From the very beginning,' she told herself, 'it has all been my fault. It is I who made him go into the Zoo. I called him mad, and mocked at him and made him suffer, when everything has been due to my ungovernable temper, my pride and my heartlessness. But all the time I have suffered, and now it is too late to do anything. He will never forgive me now. He will never bear to see me again and I must suffer always. If I had behaved differently perhaps I could have saved him and myself too. Now I have killed his love for me, and because of my folly he must suffer imprisonment and loneliness for ever, and I myself shall live miserably and never again dare hold up my head.'

Providence has not framed mankind for emotions such as these; they may be felt acutely, but in a healthy and high-spirited girl they are not of a very lasting nature.

It was only natural, then, that after giving up the greater part of the night to the bitterest self-reproach and to the completest humiliation of spirit, and after shedding enough tears to make her pillow uncomfortably damp, Miss Lackett should wake next morning in a very hopeful state of mind. She determined to visit Mr. Cromartie that afternoon, and despatched a note acquainting him with her intention in these terms:

Eaton Square.

Dear John,

You know well that the reason why I behaved badly is because I still love you. I am very much ashamed, please forgive me if you can. I must see you to-day. May I come in the afternoon? It is very important, because I don't think we can either of us continue like this much longer. I will come in the afternoon. Please consent to see me, but I will not come unless you send me word by the messenger that I may.

Yours,

Josephine Lackett.

The moment that Josephine had sent off the messenger she regretted what she had said in it, and nothing seemed to her then more certain than that her letter would exasperate Cromartie still further. The next moment she thought to herself: 'I have exposed myself to the greatest humiliation a woman can receive.' For a second or two this filled her with terror, and at that moment she would have readily killed herself. As neither poisons, poignards, pistols or precipices were within reach she did nothing, and in less than a minute the mood passed, and she said to herself:

'What does my humiliation matter? I suffered more of that last night than I can ever suffer again. Last night I humiliated myself in my own eyes. If John tries to humiliate me to-day he will find the work done. Meanwhile I must be self-controlled. I have no time to waste on my emotions; I have many things to do. I must see John, and as I am in love with him I have got to make terms with him. I have got to make a bargain with him.'

Acting on these thoughts she went out at once, meaning to walk to the Zoo without waiting any longer for the messenger boy to come back. But her mind was still busy.

'I will completely forgive him, and offer to become engaged to him secretly in return for his instantly leaving the Zoo.'

She did not reflect as she said this that nothing would be easier for her than to break off such an engagement, whereas if Cromartie once left the Gardens it was improbable that they would take him back.

But when she got to the Marble Arch she had to wait a little before crossing the road, and she noticed a man selling newspapers beside her. On the placard he carried she saw:

MAN IN THE ZOO
MAULED BY
MONKEY

For the first moment she did not connect the placard with her lover; she permitted herself to be amused at the thought of a spectator having his finger bitten, but in the next instant a doubt arose and she hurriedly bought the paper.

'This morning the "Man in the Zoo," whose real name is Mr. John Cromartie, was shockingly mauled by Daphne, the Orang in the next cage to his.' Josephine read the account of the affair right through very slowly.

It appeared that about eleven o'clock that morning Cromartie had been playing ball in his cage with the Caracal. In dodging the Caracal he had fallen heavily against the wire mesh partition separating him from the Orang. While he had rested there for a moment the spectators were horrified to see him seized by the Orang, which caught him by the hair. Mr. Cromartie had put up his hands to prevent his face being scratched, and the Orang had managed to get hold of his fingers and had cracked the bones of them. Mr. Cromartie had shown great courage and had succeeded in freeing himself before the arrival of the keeper. Two fingers were crushed and the bones fractured; he had sustained several severe scalp wounds and a scratched face. The only danger to be feared was blood poisoning, as the injuries inflicted by apes are well known to be peculiarly venomous.

On reading this Josephine suddenly remembered how the King of Greece had died from the effects of a monkey bite, and she became more and more alarmed. She called a taxi, got into it, and told the driver to take her to the Zoological Gardens as fast as he could. All the way there she was in a fever of agitation, and could settle nothing in her own mind.

Having arrived at the Zoo, she went straight to the house of the resident curator, and was just in time to see Mr. Cromartie being carried in on a stretcher, but before she could come up to it the door was shut in her face. She rang, but it was almost five minutes before the door was opened by a maidservant who took her card in, with the request that she might see the curator as she was a friend of Mr. Cromartie's. Before the maid came back, however, the curator came out, and Josephine explained her visit without any embarrassment. She was invited in, and found herself in a fine well-lit dining-room in the presence of two gentlemen in morning dress, and both with bushy eyebrows. The curator introduced her as a friend of Mr. Cromartie's, and they both gave her a very keen look and bowed.

Sir Walter Tintzel, the elder of the two, was a short man with a rather round red face; Mr. Ogilvie, a taller, youngish man, with a skin like parchment, and a glass eye into which she found herself staring. 'How is the patient?' asked Josephine, falling at once into that state of mind which is produced by the presence of distinguished medical men, and particularly surgeons, a state of mind, that is, of almost complete blankness, when however upset one may have been the moment before, one finds all emotion suspended, or swallowed up in fog. All the faculties at such a moment are concentrated on behaving with an absurd decorum.

'It is a little too early to say, Miss Lackett,' replied Sir Walter Tintzel, who was filled with curiosity to find out more about her.

'My friend Mr. Ogilvie has just amputated a finger; in my opinion it would have been running an unjustifiable risk not to have done so. There were several minor injuries, but happily they did not require such drastic measures. May I ask, Miss Lackett, without impertinence, if you have known Mr. Cromartie long? You are, I understand, a personal friend, a close and dear friend of Mr. Cromartie's.'

Miss Lackett opened her eyes rather wide at this remark, and replied:

'I was naturally anxious . . . Yes, I am an old friend of Mr. Cromartie's – and, if you like, a close friend.' She laughed. 'Is there danger of blood-poisoning?'

'There is a risk of it, but we have taken every precaution.'

'The King of Greece died of being bitten by a monkey,' cried Josephine suddenly.

'That's rubbish,' interrupted the curator, coming forward. 'Why everybody in the Gardens has been more or less seriously bitten by monkeys at some time or other. It is always happening. It's dreadful to think that the poor fellow should have lost a finger, but there's no danger.'

'You are sure there's no danger?' asked Josephine.

The curator appealed to the medical men. They allowed themselves to smile.

Josephine withdrew, and in the hall the curator said to her:

'Don't worry about him, Miss Lackett; it's a beastly thing of course to think of, but it's not serious. He isn't the King of Greece; the monkey isn't that sort of monkey even. He'll be up and about in a day or two at the most. By the way, is your father General Lackett?'

Josephine was surprised, but admitted it without hesitation.

'Oh, yes – he's an old friend of mine. Drop in one day next week to tea and see how our friend is going on.'

Josephine left in very much better spirits than she had come, and though she once or twice was troubled by the recollection of Mr. Cromartie's unconscious form, the head swathed in bandages, and the body covered with a blanket, she felt small anxiety. On the contrary, she very soon gave herself up to rosy visions of the future.

Thus nothing appeared to her to be more clear than that Mr. Cromartie would leave the Zoo, and the loss of a finger was perhaps not too high a price to pay for restoring him to ordinary ways, or perhaps she might say not too great a punishment for conduct such as his had been.

And it crossed her mind also that now there was no need for her to humble herself to Cromartie, for he would leave the Zoo and become reconciled to her now as a matter of course. It was for her to forgive him! She had had a narrow escape. What a weak position she might have been in had she seen him before the ape bit him! How strong a position she now occupied! She must, she reflected, take this lesson to heart and never act hurriedly on the impulse of the moment, otherwise she would give John every advantage and there would be no dealing with him at all. Next she recollected the letter she had sent him, and spent a little while trying to recall the exact terms of it. When she remembered that she had said that she was ashamed and had asked to be forgiven, she bit her lips with vexation, but the next moment she stopped short and said aloud: 'How unworthy this is of you! How petty! How vulgar!'

And she remembered at that moment all the vulgar and horrible things she had felt when she had first learnt that John had gone to the Zoo, and how much ashamed she was of them afterwards, and how hatefully she had behaved on both of her visits to him. She told herself then that she ought to be ashamed, ought to ask forgiveness, and that she ought to be thankful that she had done so in her letter, but in the next instant she was saying to herself: 'All the same, it won't do to put myself at his mercy. I must keep the upper hand or my life won't be worth living.' And after that her mind raced off again to visions of the future in which John was rewarded with her hand and they took a country house. Her father was an authority on fishponds and trout streams. He and Cromartie would of course lay out a fishpond. Perhaps there would be a moat round the house. But the figure who bent over her father's shoulder at breakfast, pushing away the egg-boiling machine to look at a plan of the new trout hatchery, that figure was a very different person from Mr. Cromartie the mutilated, monkey-bitten man in the Zoo.

When Josephine got home she found a note which had been left for her, but which was not in Mr. Cromartie's handwriting.

It ran as follows:

Infirmary, Zoo.

Dear Josephine,

Your note has come by the messenger. I shall not be free to see you this afternoon, which relieves me from making the decision not to do so. You say that the reason you behave cruelly to me is because you love me. It is because I know that, that I have tried to do without your love. I think you are a character who will always torture the people you love. I cannot bear pain well; that alone makes us unsuited to each other. It is the principal reason why I never wish to see you again.

You are mistaken when you say that you have something of the first importance to tell me. Unless it is something to do with the arrangements which the Zoo authorities make with regard to the Ape-house, it cannot be of importance to me.

Please believe that I bear you no resentment for the past; indeed I still love you, but I mean what I say.

Yours ever,
John Cromartie.

When Josephine had read this letter over twice and had realised that it must have been written *after* he had been bitten by the ape, and just before his finger was cut off, she gave up her hopes.

Everything she had been feeling was revealed as ridiculous folly. If John could write like that at the moment when he must have been most wishing to escape from confinement, she saw that her plans for his regeneration were impossible. She went up to her room and lay down. All was lost.

That morning Mr. Cromartie had taken his breakfast of rolls, butter, Oxford marmalade, and coffee as usual. When it had been cleared away he began to play ball with the Caracal.

For this purpose he used an ordinary tennis ball, and throwing it on the floor of his cage, made it bounce on to the netting and back to him. The game therefore resembled fives, the object, however, being, on his part, to prevent the Caracal intercepting the ball, which, by the way, he was rarely able to do more than three or four times running, for the cat was very quick on its legs and had a good eye.

After they had been playing for about ten minutes Mr. Cromartie slipped backwards in taking a ball which bounced high, and fell heavily against the wire-netting wall of his cage. Before he could get his balance he felt himself taken hold of by the hair, and understood at once that it was his neighbour the Orang who had got him in its clutches. The brute then got a finger as far as Mr. Cromartie's ear and slit it through, though not injuring the drum. Mr. Cromartie managed to turn his head then in order to see his assailant, and found his face was now exposed, and his forehead was scratched. To protect himself he put one hand in front of his face, and was pushing himself away from the netting with the other when the Orang caught hold of two of his fingers in its teeth. The pain of this made him jerk his head free, and the lock of hair by which the Orang held him came right out of his scalp.

The ape still held on to his fingers like a bulldog. Just then his Caracal, which had been dodging about between his legs, got one paw through the netting and raked the Orang's thighs with his claws, but the ape did not leave go even then. Mr. Cromartie, who had a very cool head for a man in such a situation, took out a couple of wax vestas from his pocket, struck them on his heel, and thrust the flaring fusees through the wire into the ape's muzzle and in that way made him leave go his hold at once.

This circumstance of his feeling for the fusees in his pocket while the ape was slowly grinding his fingers to a mere pulp very greatly impressed the spectators, who beyond shouting for assistance were powerless to do anything. No less remarkable was the way in which, directly he was free, he pulled away the Caracal from the netting before the ape could catch hold of him, and this though the cat was beside itself with the fury of the fight. But strangely enough in doing this he did not get scratched, either because he pulled him off by the scruff with his uninjured hand and carried him right out of the cage, or because the Caracal knew him even at that moment.

Collins arrived just as this happened and the shock was almost too much for him; it was remarked that he was deathly white and could scarcely speak. Mr. Cromartie was covered with blood, blood pouring from his ear and his fingers, and all his hair matted with blood, but he came back at once after locking up his Caracal, to show the spectators that he was not badly hurt; they for their part clapped their hands with joy, either because they were glad to see him

escape, or because they were grateful for having been presented with such an unusual spectacle for nothing.

Cromartie then went back to his inner room and Collins led him off at once to the infirmary, where he was given first aid. It was some little while after this that he received Josephine's letter and dictated an answer for the messenger to take to her. There was some little delay in the messenger getting to him

Directly he had despatched the letter he was anaesthetised and the third finger of his right hand amputated.

After the operation and before he had regained consciousness, he was taken to the house of the curator, who had decided that he would be more comfortable there than anywhere else. Although at the time Mr. Cromartie had behaved with perfect composure and had borne his injuries without flinching, not only at the time of the assault, but for over three hours afterwards, and had been able to compose a letter during that time as if nothing had happened, he had received a great nervous shock the effects of which only became apparent next day. He spent a very disturbed night, but in the morning was much better; ate an ordinary breakfast but did not get up, and Sir Walter Tintzel, who visited him about eleven o'clock, was sanguine and predicted a rapid recovery. In the afternoon he was restless and suffered acutely, and as evening came on his temperature rose rapidly. That night he was in a condition of fitful delirium, occasionally falling asleep and waking up with nightmares which persisted even when he appeared to be wide awake.

On the second day the fever increased and blood-poisoning in an acute form was recognised, but the patient was altogether rational in his mind. On the third day the symptoms of blood-poisoning were more pronounced. The patient fell into a delirium which lasted without intermission for the following three days. Most of the feverish hallucinations which filled his mind then passed completely away when he recovered consciousness. Yet Mr. Cromartie had a clear and vivid memory of one of them. This was, he knew, nothing but a dream, yet it seemed but to have just happened to him, and the dream or vision was singular enough for it to be put down here.

In the Strand people were hurrying along in little crowds like gusts of dirty smoke that was blown at intervals in wisps across the road. They were all coming towards him as he walked down from Somerset House towards Trafalgar Square. No one was walking the same way that he was, and none of the people he met brushed against him or even looked at him, but they melted away to right and left and so let him pass by. Sometimes when a band of them passed him he caught a whiff of their odour, and the smell sickened him.

They were frightened, they hurried by, but he was thinking of that great man Sir Christopher Wren, who had planned the street he was then walking in. But nobody cared, nobody had built it, though the plans were all there rolled up and ready, and just as good to-day as they were in the reign of King Charles II.

He lifted up his head presently, and up in the sky a white streak was being deliberately drawn. It was an aeroplane writing advertisements. So he stood still in the middle of the hurrying crowds to watch it; now he could just see the tiny aeroplane like a little brown insect. Slowly in the sky a long straight line was drawn and then a loop – surely it must be the figure 6. And then the aeroplane stopped throwing out smoke and became almost invisible as it went off tittering across the sky.

The numeral swelled and grew and was being slowly blown away when all of a sudden another white streak appeared and the aeroplane was drawing something else. But as he watched he was aware that after all it was the same thing again, another 6, and when it had done that the aeroplane mounted again into the sky and drew another 6, but already its first work was undone by the wind and in a few moments there was nothing to be seen in the sky but a few wisps of smoke.

For a second or two Cromartie felt himself rocking in the aeroplane, which went humming away across the sky before falling again sideways like a snipe bleating; that was only a moment, as when you shut your eyes and fancy that you can feel the earth spinning in space, and then Cromartie was walking out of the Strand into Trafalgar Square. It was empty, and he looked at the Nelson monument with wonder. Landseer's great beasts planted their feet flat down before them. What were they, he wondered? Lions or Leopards, or perhaps Bears? He could not say. And suddenly he saw that his right hand was bleeding and his fingers gone. A great crowd had entered the Square; the fountains were playing, the sun was shining, and he got on to a scarlet omnibus. But very soon he saw that the people were whispering together on the omnibus and they were all looking at him, and he knew that it was because they saw his wounded hand. He put his other hand up to his forehead and there was blood on that also. He was afraid then of the people on the bus and so he got out. But wherever he wandered the people stopped and stared at him and whispered, and as he walked among them they drew aside and formed into little groups and gazed after him as he went by, and it was because they knew him by the wounds on his head and on his hand.

They were all of them muttering and looking at him with hatred, but something restrained them, so that though their eyes were like sharp daggers they were one and all afraid to point their fingers . . .

He was going to vote. He would cast his vote. Nothing should stop him. At last he saw the two entrances to the underground voting hall with Ladies written over one and Gentlemen written over the other, and he went downstairs. But when he asked the attendant for his voting card the man took down a large book bound in lambskin with the wool left on, and turned over several pages and looked down them. At last he said: 'But your name is not written in the Book of Life, Mr. Cromartie. You must give up your secret, you know, if you wish to be registered.' When he heard this Mr. Cromartie felt sick, and he noticed the smell that came from all the other voters in their ballot boxes; he hesitated, and at last he said:

'But if I do not give up my secret may I not vote?'

'No, Mr. Cromartie. Nobody can vote who does not give up his secret, that is called the secrecy of the ballot – but it is out of the question for you to vote, anyhow . . . you bear the Mark of the Beast.'

And Mr. Comartie looked at his hand and felt his forehead and saw that he did indeed bear the Mark of the Beast where it had bitten him, and he knew that he was an outcast. That was what everybody had whispered. He would not give up his secret so he was rejected by mankind and hated by them, for he frightened them. They were all alike, they had no secrets, but he had kept his and now the Beast had set its Mark upon him, and he seemed terrible to them all, and he himself was afraid. 'The Beast has set his Mark on me,' he said to himself. 'It will slowly eat me up. I cannot escape now, and one thing is as bad as another. On the whole I would rather the Beast slowly ate me up than give up so much, and the stench of my fellows disgusts me.'

And then he heard the Beast moving restlessly behind some partition; he heard the rustling of straw and the great creature slowly licking itself all over; and then its smell, sweet, and warm, and awful, swallowed him up, and he lay quite still on the floor of the cage, listening to its tail going thump, thump, thump on the floor beside him. Terror could go no further, and at last he opened his eyes and slowly understood that it was his own heart which was beating and no beast's tail, and all about him there were clean sheets and flowers and a smell of iodoform. But his fear lasted for half that day.

In a fortnight Mr. Cromartie was pronounced out of danger, but he continued in so weak a state for some time afterwards that he was not allowed to receive any visitors, so that although Josephine called every day it was only to hear the latest news of how he had passed the night, and to leave flowers for the sickroom.

In the following weeks Mr. Cromartie made a rapid recovery; that is to say, though by no means restored to his ordinary health, he was able first to get up for an hour in the middle of the day, and then to go for a short walk round the Gardens.

The doctors attending upon him suggested at this time that an entire change of scene would be beneficial, and the curator, far from putting any obstacles in the way of this, frequently urged the patient to go for a month's holiday to Cornwall. But in this he was met by a steady and obstinate refusal, or rather by complete passivity and non-resistance. Mr. Cromartie refused to take a holiday. He declined to go away anywhere by himself, though he added that he was completely at the curator's disposal and prepared to go to any place where he was sent in charge of a keeper. After some days, during which the curator proposed first one scheme and then another, the plan of Mr. Cromartie's being sent away was abandoned. In the first place it was difficult to spare a keeper, or for that matter to find a suitable man among the staff to go with Mr. Cromartie, and it was difficult to find a suitable place where they should be sent.

But the chief reason why these schemes were given up was because of the apathetic and even hostile attitude which the invalid adopted to them, and because it occurred to the curator that this hostility was perhaps not without a reason.

And indeed there is no doubt that Mr. Cromartie felt that if he once took such a holiday as had been suggested he would find it very much harder to go back into captivity at the end of it, and he opposed it because he was resolved not to escape from what he conceived were his obligations.

It was therefore decided that Mr. Cromartie should go straight back to his cage, though it was impressed upon him that he would not be expected to be on view to the public any longer than he wished, and that he must lie down to rest in his inner room for two or three hours every day.

In this way, and by taking him for motor-car drives for a couple of hours or so after dark, it was hoped that he would be able to regain his accustomed health and shake off that state of apathy which seemed his most alarming symptom to the medical men who attended him.

But before Cromartie went back to his old quarters he was to hear a piece of news from the curator which concerned him very closely, though he did not at first realise the full significance of it.

The curator was so confused in imparting this information,

and so apologetic, and occupied so much time with a preamble explaining how much the Zoological Society felt themselves indebted to him, that Mr. Cromartie had some difficulty in following what he said, but at last he got at the gist of it, and the long and the short of the matter was: The experiment of exhibiting a man had been a much greater success than any of the Committee had dared to hope; such a success, indeed, that it had decided to follow it up by having a second man, a negro. It had actually engaged him two or three days since, and had installed him only that day. The intention of the Committee was eventually to establish a 'Man-house' which should contain specimens of all the different races of mankind, with a Bushman, South Sea Islanders, etc., in native costume, but such a collection could of course only be formed gradually and as occasion offered.

The embarrassment of the poor curator as he made these revelations was so extreme that Cromartie could only think of how best to set him once more at his ease, and though he had a very distinct moment of annoyance when he heard of the negro, yet he suppressed it completely. When the curator had been persuaded that Cromartie bore him no grudge for these innovations, nay more, that he was perfectly indifferent to them, his joy and relief were as overwhelming as his distress and embarrassment had been before.

First he blew out a great breath, and mopped his forehead with a big silk handkerchief; then, his honest face quite transformed with happiness, he seized Cromartie by the hand, and then by the lapel, and laughed again and again while he explained that he had opposed the project with all his might because he was sure Cromartie would not like it, and after he had been overruled he had not known how to break the news to him. He vowed he had not slept for two nights thinking about it, but now when he learnt that Cromartie actually approved of the plan, he felt a new man. 'I am the biggest fool in the world,' said he; 'my imagination runs away with me. I am always thinking of how other people are going to be upset, and then it turns out that they don't give a row of pins about the whole affair and I am the only person who feels upset at all ... all on account of somebody else ... Ha! Ha! Ha! It has been just like that over and over again with my wife. It is always happening to me. Well now I'll go full blast ahead with the new "Man-house," because, you know, it's a damned good notion. I felt that the whole time, but I couldn't get it out of my head that it was unfair to you.'

But Mr. Cromartie did not share his enthusiasm; he merely repeated to himself, as he had done so often before, that he intended observing his side of the contract so long as the Zoo kept its own, and that there was nothing in all this which infringed or invalidated the contract in any way. But when Mr. Cromartie went into his cage he saw a black man in the cage next door – he was brushing a black bowler hat – it came as a great shock to Mr. Cromartie to realise that this man was the neighbour about whom the curator had spoken. This negro was almost coal black, a jovial fellow, dressed in a striped pink and green shirt, a mustard-coloured suit, and patent leather boots. When he saw Mr. Cromartie he at once wheeled round, and saying 'The interesting invalid has arrived,' walked up to the partition separating him from Cromartie and said to him: 'Allow me to welcome you back to what is now the Man-house. If I may introduce myself, Joe Tennison: I am delighted to meet you, Mr. Cromartie, it is a real pleasure to have a man next door.' Cromartie bowed stiffly and said 'Good afternoon' very awkwardly, but the negro was not abashed, and leaned against the wire partition between them so that it bulged.

'They are going to clear all that poor trash away now,' he said, pointing at the Chimpanzee beyond Cromartie. 'They isn't to be kept with us any more, nasty jealous brutes; bite your fingers off if they catch you.'

Cromartie turned and looked at the Chimpanzee; it had always seemed to him rather a pathetic beast, but how much more so now while his new neighbour Tennison was speaking of it! And not for the first time he felt a friendly sympathy for the ugly little ape. Indeed he would far rather have seen the savage old Orang back in her place than have this insufferably verbose fellow patronising the animals near him.

For the moment Cromartie was quite at a loss, and had no idea what to reply to the stream of Mr. Tennison's remarks. He had said nothing at all when a minute or two later he was relieved by the arrival of Collins with his Caracal, which had been sent back to his old cage in the cat-house after Mr. Cromartie's injuries.

The pleasure of the two friends at once more being together was unbounded, and was shown by each of them very strongly after his own fashion. For at first the Caracal trotted up to Cromartie debonairly enough, as if he were just come to give him a sniff, then he began purring loudly and rubbed himself a score of times against Cromartie's legs, winding himself about them, and finally he sprang right up into his friend's arms, licked his face and his hair, and curled up for a moment or two as if he would sleep there; but no, this was not for long, for he sprang down again. Then he began trotting round the cage, sniffed in the corners, leapt on the table and made certain that all was well.

When Joe Tennison called to him, the Caracal passed by without giving him a glance, and it was just the same with his friend too, for when Cromartie heard the negro begin talking to him he just nodded his head and went into his inner room. But once there Mr. Cromartie reflected that this negro was to be his companion and neighbour for some years, and it would never do to run away from him every time he spoke. Somehow he must make Tennison respect his privacy without making an enemy of him, and at that moment Mr. Cromartie saw no way of doing this. However, he took down a book of Waley's poems translated from the Chinese, and went back into his cage with it in his hand, and then sat down and began reading.

He lives in thick forests, deep among the hills,
Or houses in the clefts of sharp, precipitous rocks;
Alert and agile is his nature, nimble are his wits;
Swift are his contortions,

Apt to every need,
Whether he climbs tall tree-stems of a hundred feet,
Or sways on the shuddering shoulder of a long bough.
Before him, the dark gullies of unfathomable streams;
Behind, the silent hollows of the lonely hills.
Twigs and tendrils are his rocking-chairs,
On rungs of rotting wood he trips
Up perilous places; sometimes, leap after leap,
Like lightning flits through the woods.
Sometimes he saunters with a sad, forsaken air;
Then suddenly peeps round
Beaming with satisfaction. Up he springs,
Leaps and prances, whoops and scampers on his way.
Up cliffs he scrambles, up pointed rocks,
Dances on shale that shifts or twigs that snap,
Suddenly swerves and lightly passes . . .
Oh, what tongue could unravel
The tale of all his tricks?
Alas, one trait
With the human tribe he shares; their sweets his sweet,
Their bitter is his bitter. Off sugar from the vat
Of brewers' dregs he loves to sup.
So men put wine where he will pass.
How he races to the bowl!
How nimbly licks and swills!
Now he staggers, feels dazed and foolish,
Darkness falls upon his eyes . . .
He sleeps and knows no more.
Up steal the trappers, catch him by the mane,
Then to a string or ribbon tie him, lead him home;
Tether him in the stable or lock him in the yard;
Where faces all day long
Gaze, gape, gasp at him and will not go away.

Joe Tennison came up three or four times while he was
reading and began a conversation, but Cromartie ignored his
remarks and did not even lift his head, but just read quietly
on.

Fortunately there were a great many of the public come to see their old favourite Mr. Cromartie now he was back, and to have a look at the new black man also, about whom there was nearly as much discussion as there ever had been about Cromartie himself.

The presence of the public was lucky for two reasons; firstly, it served to distract Joe Tennison by giving him that which he most wanted in life – an audience; and secondly, Mr. Cromartie was able, by totally ignoring spectators, to show him that that was his ordinary method of conducting himself. There was therefore no reason why the negro should feel himself insulted by being treated as if he did not exist. And here I should explain that Mr. Cromartie had no objection to his neighbour as a negro, and no particular prejudice against persons of that colour. Mr. Tennison was indeed the first negro to whom he had spoken. At the same time the fellow aroused a strong feeling of dislike, and this aversion was one which steadily increased as time went on.

The next day Mr. Cromartie found Josephine Lackett waiting for him when he first went into his cage after breakfast. She was standing a little distance off looking out of the door of the Ape-house (to give it its old name), and Cromartie called out to her before he reflected on what he was doing: 'Josephine! Josephine! What are you doing there?'

She turned round and came towards him, and the sight of her so much affected Mr. Cromartie that for some time he did not trust himself to speak again, and when he did so it was more tenderly than he had done since his captivity. But Josephine on her part could not for some time get used to the presence of Mr. Tennison, who sat lolling in a deck chair within a few feet of them and kept putting his gold-rimmed eyeglass in his eye to stare at her, and then letting it fall out, as if he had not quite learnt the trick of it, which was indeed the case, as he had only bought it a week before.

For some little time then Josephine found herself with nothing to say except to congratulate John on his recovery, and to tell him how glad she was that he was well again.

Then she thanked him for calling to her and letting her speak to him.

'Don't behave like a goose, Josephine,' said John Cromartie. Then guessing why she was constrained, he said: 'My dear Josephine, do ignore him as I do.'

But Josephine did not speak, and just then in strolled the Caracal, having just completed his morning toilet.

'I paid your cat several visits while you were ill,' said Josephine. 'He seemed very unhappy and would not take much notice of me. I think he is rather shy of women, and is not used to them.'

Mr. Cromartie nodded. He was glad Josephine had gone to see the Caracal, but he knew that she had wasted her time; he did not care for the people who came and gazed into his cage from the outside. Suddenly he heard Josephine say: 'John, I must see you in private. I must talk to you, because I cannot go on like this. You cannot go on shirking things any longer.'

'What do you mean?'

'I mean that you must recognise that we are bound up with each other. I don't mind *what* you decide to do, but you must do something. I cannot go on living like this any longer. Please arrange somehow for us to see each other and talk it over.'

It was Cromartie now who was embarrassed and shy; Cromartie who could not talk simply about what he felt, at least not for a considerable time. At last, however, he got out a few disconnected remarks, saying he was very sorry but he could do nothing then, and that he was not a free agent. But in the end he got more confidence and looked Josephine straight in the eyes and said: 'My dear, it's quite inevitable that both of us should be unhappy. I love you, if you want me to put it in that way. I cannot ever forget you, and now you seem to be feeling the same for me, and you too must expect to be very unhappy. I only hope your feeling for me will wear off. I daresay it will in time, and I hope my feeling for you will also. Until then we must try and be resigned.'

'I am not resigned,' said Josephine. 'I'm going to get savage about it, or go mad or something.'

'It's the greatest mistake for us to stir up each other's feelings,' said Cromartie rather roughly. 'That's the worst thing we can either of us do, the most unkind thing. No, the only thing for you to do is to forget me, the only hope for me is to forget you.'

'That's impossible; it's worse when we don't see each other,' said Josephine.

Just then they realised that several people had come into the Ape-house and were hesitating to interrupt their conversation.

'It's a bad business,' said Cromartie, 'a damned bad business,' and at these words Josephine went away. He turned away and sat down, but a moment later he heard a loud 'Excuse me, Sah. Excuse an intrusion, but I believe, Sah, that your young lady friend's Christian name is Josephine. That is a remarkable coincidence! for my own name, you know, is Joseph. Joseph and Josephine.'

If, on hearing this remark, Mr. Cromartie gave Tennison any encouragement to continue, it was quite accidental. At the moment he was feeling faint, and only by an effort of will continued standing where he was without clutching hold of the bars.

'Are you interested in the girls?' asked the negro. 'They come and watch me all the morning, and they do stare so . . . he, he, he.'

'No, I'm not interested,' said Mr. Cromartie. Nobody could have mistaken the desperate sincerity in his voice.

'I'm glad to hear that,' said Tennison, at once restored to his former heartiness and buoyancy of manner.

'That is how I feel myself, just how I feel. I have no interest in women at all. Only my poor old mammy, my old black mammy, she was of the very best, the very best she was. A mother is the best friend you have through life – the best friend you can make. My mother was ignorant, she could not read, neither could she write, but she knew almost all of the whole Bible by heart, and I first learnt of Salvation from my mother's lips. When I was five years old she taught me the

Holy Words of Glory, and I repeated them after her text by text. She was the best friend I shall ever have.

'But other women – no, sir. I have no use for them. They are just a temptation in a man's life, a temptation to make him forget his true manhood. And the worst of it is that the more you shun them the more they do run after you. That's a fact.

'No, I am very much safer and better off here shut up alongside of you, with this wire-netting and bars to fence off the women, and I guess you feel the same way as I do. Don't you, Mr. Cromartie?'

Cromartie suddenly looked up and saw the person who had been addressing him. 'Who are you?' he asked, and then, looking rather wildly, he walked out of his cage into his back room, where he lay down feeling very exhausted.

He was still very weak from his illness, and the close atmosphere of the Ape-house gave him a headache. Every moment he had now to exercise self-control, and it was more and more exhausting for him to do so. Very often he did what he did on this occasion, and this was to lie down to rest in his back room and then burst into tears, quite without any restraint, and though he laughed at himself afterwards, the act of weeping comforted him, although it left him weaker than before and more inclined to weep again.

But the pricks and troubles of the outside world meant very little to Mr. Cromartie just then. He could not help thinking the whole time of Josephine.

For so long he had believed that there were so many insuperable obstacles which would prevent them ever being happy together, that the additional fact of his being shut up in the Zoo was a relief to him. But now that he felt so weak it was an extra strain, and especially now as he was beginning to wonder if Josephine and he could not be happy together for a little while.

He still knew that they were too proud to endure each other for very long, but could they not have a week or a month or even a year of happiness together?

Perhaps they might, but anyhow it wasn't possible, and

here he was locked up in a cage, with a nigger waiting outside to talk some disgusting trash at him and wear out his patience.

But as a matter of fact, when Cromartie pulled himself together once more and went out into his cage Joe Tennison did not address him – that is, not directly. But he was as tiresome as he had been before, but now it was in a different way.

When Cromartie had settled down and had been reading for a little while, there were no visitors for two or three minutes, and then he heard the negro speaking to himself as he gazed in his direction.

'Poor fellow! Poor young fellow! The women do make hay with a man, they do. I've been through it all . . . I know all about it . . . Oh, gracious, yes. Love! Love is the very devil. And that poor young man is certainly in love. Nobody can cheer him up. Nobody can do anything except her that caused the trouble in his heart. There's nothing I can do for him now except just to pretend to notice nothing, the same as I always do.' At this point the speaker was distracted by the arrival of a party of visitors who stopped outside his cage, but thereafter Mr. Cromartie adopted the same method to the negro that he had always adopted to the public. That is to say, he ignored his existence and contrived never to meet his eyes, and never took the least notice of what he said.

The next morning, while Cromartie was playing with his Caracal, with a ball, as he had been accustomed to do before the Orang had taken advantage of him, he heard Josephine's voice calling to him.

He threw the ball to his friend the bounding, tasselled cat, and went straight to her, and without waiting for any greeting she said to him:

'John, I love you, and I must see you alone at once. I must come into your cage and talk to you there.'

'No, Josephine, don't – that's not possible,' said Cromartie. 'I can't go on seeing you like this even, and surely you see that if you were to come into my cage I could not bear it after you had gone away.'

'But I don't want to go away,' said Josephine.

'If you were ever to come inside my cage you would have to stay for ever,' said Cromartie. He had recovered himself now, his moment of weakness was past. 'And if you don't decide to do that, I don't think we can go on seeing each other at all. I think I shall die if I see you like this. We can never be happy together.'

'Well, we had better be unhappy together than unhappy apart,' said Josephine. She had suddenly begun to cry.

'My darling creature,' said Cromartie, 'it's all a silly mistake; but we will arrange things somehow. I'll get the curator to have you in the next cage to me instead of that damned nigger, and we shall see each other all the time.'

Josephine shook her head vigorously to get the tears out of her eyes, like a dog that has been swimming.

'No, that won't do,' she declared angrily, 'that won't do at all. It has got to be the same cage as yours or I won't live in a cage at all. I haven't come here to live in a cage by myself. I'll share yours and be damned to everyone else.'

She gave an angry laugh and shook her yellow hair back. Her eyes sparkled with tears, but she looked steadily at Cromartie. 'Damn other people,' she repeated; 'I care for nobody in the world but you, John, and if we are going to be put in a cage and persecuted, we must just bear it. I hate them all, and I'm going to be happy with you in spite of them. Nobody can make me feel ashamed now. I can't help being myself and I will be myself.'

'Darling,' said Cromartie, 'you would be wretched here. It's awful; you mustn't think of it. I have a much more sensible plan. I can't ask them to let me go. Anyhow I shan't do that. But I am still so feeble that I can easily make myself really ill again, and then I think they will let me go and we can get married.'

'That won't do,' said Josephine. 'We can't wait any longer, and you would die if you tried that. There was nothing about your not being allowed to marry in the contract when you came here, was there?' she asked. 'You have only got to tell them that you are going to get married to-day, and that your wife is ready to live in your cage.'

During this conversation several people had come into the Ape-house, and after looking at Josephine in a highly scandalised manner had gone out again, but now Collins came in. He looked rather puzzled and awkward when he saw Josephine, but she turned to him at once and said:

'Mr. Cromartie and I wish to see the curator; will you please find him and ask him to come here?'

'Very good,' said Collins; then catching sight of Joe Tennison gazing at Cromartie and the lady from a distance of three feet, with his yellow eyeballs almost popping out of his sooty face, he sternly ordered him to go into the back room of his cage.

'Oh, I can tell you something, I can tell you what you'd never believe,' cried Joe, but Collins silently pointed his finger at him, and the nigger jumped up and slowly beat a retreat into his own quarters.

Ten minutes later the curator came in.

'Come round to the back where we can talk more conveniently, Miss Lackett,' he said. Then he unlocked the door of the inner cage or den and Josephine walked in. They sat down.

'I have asked Miss Lackett to marry me, and have been accepted,' said Cromartie rather stiffly. 'I was anxious to tell you at once, so as to make arrangements with regard to the ceremony, which of course we wish to be carried out as privately as possible, and at once. After our marriage my wife is prepared to live with me in this cage, unless of course you arrange for us to have other quarters.'

The curator suddenly laughed, a loud, good-natured, hearty laugh. To Cromartie it seemed a piece of brutality, to Josephine a menace. They both frowned, and drew slightly together waiting for the worst.

'I ought to explain to you,' the curator began, 'that the committee has already considered what to do in the event of such a contingency as this occurring.

'It is impossible, for various reasons, for us to keep married couples in the Man-house, and we decided that in the event of your mentioning marriage, Mr. Cromartie, that we should consider our contract with you at an end. In other words you are free to go, and in fact I am now going to turn you out.'

As he said these words the curator rose and opened the door. For a moment the happy couple hesitated; they looked at each other and then walked out of the cage together, but Josephine kept hold of her man as they did so. The curator slammed the door and locked it on the forgotten Caracal, and then said:

'Cromartie, I congratulate you very heartily; and my dear Miss Lackett, you have chosen a man for whom all of us here have the very greatest respect and admiration. I hope you will be happy with him.'

Hand in hand Josephine and John hurried through the Gardens. They did not stop to look at dogs or foxes, or wolves or tigers, they raced past the lion house and the cattle sheds, and without glancing at the pheasants or a lonely peacock, slipped through the turnstile into Regent's Park. There, still hand in hand, they passed unnoticed into the crowd. Nobody looked at them, nobody recognised them. The crowd was chiefly composed of couples like themselves.

LADY INTO FOX

TO
DUNCAN GRANT

Mr. and Mrs. Tebrick at Home

LADY INTO FOX

WONDERFUL OR SUPERNATURAL events are not so uncommon, rather they are irregular in their incidence. Thus there may be not one marvel to speak of in a century, and then often enough comes a plentiful crop of them; monsters of all sorts swarm suddenly upon the earth, comets blaze in the sky, eclipses frighten nature, meteors fall in rain, while mermaids and sirens beguile, and sea-serpents engulf every passing ship, and terrible cataclysms beset humanity.

But the strange event which I shall here relate came alone, unsupported, without companions into a hostile world, and for that very reason claimed little of the general attention of mankind. For the sudden changing of Mrs. Tebrick into a vixen is an established fact which we may attempt to account for as we will. Certainly it is in the explanation of the fact, and the reconciling of it with our general notions that we shall find most difficulty, and not in accepting for true a story which is so fully proved, and that not by one witness but by a dozen, all respectable, and with no possibility of collusion between them.

But here I will confine myself to an exact narrative of the event and all that followed on it. Yet I would not dissuade any of my readers from attempting an explanation of this seeming miracle because up till now none has been found which is entirely satisfactory. What adds to the difficulty to my mind is that the metamorphosis occurred when Mrs. Tebrick was a full-grown woman, and that it happened suddenly in so short a space of time. The sprouting of a tail, the gradual extension of hair all over the body, the slow change of the whole anatomy by a process of growth, though it would have been monstrous, would not have been so difficult to reconcile to our ordinary conceptions, particularly had it happened in a young child.

But here we have something very different. A grown lady is changed straightway into a fox. There is no explaining that away by any natural philosophy. The materialism of our age will not help us here. It is indeed *a miracle*; something from outside our world altogether; an event which we would willingly accept if we were to meet it invested with the authority of Divine Revelation in the scriptures, but which we are not prepared to encounter almost in our time, happening in Oxfordshire amongst our neighbours.

The only things which go any way towards an explanation of it are but guesswork, and I give them more because I would not conceal anything, than because I think they are of any worth.

Mrs. Tebrick's maiden name was certainly Fox, and it is possible that such a miracle happening before, the family may have gained their name as a *soubriquet* on that account. They were an ancient family, and have had their seat at Tangley Hall time out of mind. It is also true that there was a half-tame fox once upon a time chained up at Tangley Hall in the inner yard, and I have heard many speculative wiseacres in the public-houses turn that to great account – though they could not but admit that 'there was never one there in Miss Silvia's time.' At first I was inclined to think that Silvia Fox, having once hunted when she was a child of ten and having been blooded, might furnish more of an explanation. It seems she took great fright or disgust at it, and vomited after it was done. But now I do not see that it has much bearing on the miracle itself, even though we know that after that she always spoke of the 'poor foxes' when a hunt was stirring and never rode to hounds till after her marriage when her husband persuaded her to it.

She was married in the year 1879 to Mr. Richard Tebrick, after a short courtship, and went to live after their honeymoon at Rylands, near Stokoe, Oxon. One point indeed I have not been able to ascertain and that is how they first became acquainted. Tangley Hall is over thirty miles from Stokoe, and is extremely remote. Indeed to this day there is no proper road to it, which is all the more remarkable as it is the principal, and indeed the only, manor house for several miles round.

Whether it was from a chance meeting on the roads, or less romantic but more probable, by Mr. Tebrick becoming acquainted with her uncle, a minor canon at Oxford, and thence being invited by him to visit Tangley Hall, it is impossible to say. But however they became acquainted the marriage was a very happy one. The bride was in her twenty-third year. She was small, with remarkably small hands and feet. It is perhaps worth noting that there was nothing at all foxy or vixenish in her appearance. On the contrary, she was a more than ordinarily beautiful and agreeable woman. Her eyes were of a clear hazel but exceptionally brilliant, her hair dark, with a shade of red in it, her skin brownish, with a few dark freckles and little moles. In manner she was reserved almost to shyness, but perfectly self-possessed, and perfectly well-bred.

She had been strictly brought up by a woman of excellent principles and considerable attainments, who died a year or so before the marriage. And owing to the circumstance that her mother had been dead many years, and her father bedridden, and not altogether rational for a little while before his death, they had few visitors but her uncle. He often stopped with them a month or two at a stretch, particularly in winter, as he was fond of shooting snipe, which are plentiful in the valley there. That she did not grow up a country hoyden is to be explained by the strictness of her governess and the influence of her uncle. But perhaps living in so wild a place gave her some disposition to wildness, even in spite of her religious upbringing. Her old nurse said: 'Miss Silvia was always a little wild at heart,' though if this was true it was never seen by anyone else except her husband.

On one of the first days of the year 1880, in the early afternoon, husband and wife went for a walk in the copse on the little hill above Rylands. They were still at this time like lovers in their behaviour and were always together. While they were walking they heard the hounds and later the huntsman's horn in the distance. Mr. Tebrick had persuaded her to hunt on Boxing Day, but with great difficulty, and she had not enjoyed it (though of hacking she was fond enough).

Hearing the hunt, Mr. Tebrick quickened his pace so as to reach the edge of the copse, where they might get a good view of the hounds if they came that way. His wife hung back, and he, holding her hand, began almost to drag her. Before they gained the edge of the copse she suddenly snatched her hand away from his very violently and cried out, so that he instantly turned his head.

Where his wife had been the moment before was a small fox, of a very bright red. It looked at him very beseechingly, advanced towards him a pace or two, and he saw at once that his wife was looking at him from the animal's eyes. You may well think if he were aghast: and so maybe was his lady at finding herself in that shape, so they did nothing for nearly half-an-hour but stare at each other, he bewildered, she asking him with her eyes as if indeed she spoke to him: 'What am I now become? Have pity on me, husband, have pity on me for I am your wife.'

So that with his gazing on her and knowing her well, even in such a shape, yet asking himself at every moment: 'Can it be she? Am I not dreaming?' and her beseeching and lastly fawning on him and seeming to tell him that it was she indeed, they came at last together and he took her in his arms. She lay very close to him, nestling under his coat and fell to licking his face, but never taking her eyes from his.

The husband all this while kept turning the thing in his head and gazing on her, but he could make no sense of what had happened, but only comforted himself with the hope that this was but a momentary change, and that presently she would turn back again into the wife that was one flesh with him.

One fancy that came to him, because he was so much more like a lover than a husband, was that it was his fault, and this because if anything dreadful happened he could never blame her but himself for it.

So they passed a good while, till at last the tears welled up in the poor fox's eyes and she began weeping (but quite in silence), and she trembled too as if she were in a fever. At this he could not contain his own tears, but sat down on the ground and sobbed for a great while, but between his sobs kissing her quite as if she had been a woman, and not caring in his grief that he was kissing a fox on the muzzle.

They sat thus till it was getting near dusk, when he recollected himself, and the next thing was that he must somehow hide her, and then bring her home.

He waited till it was quite dark that he might the better bring her into her own house without being seen, and buttoned her inside his topcoat, nay, even in his passion tearing open his waistcoat and his shirt that she might lie the closer to his heart. For when we are overcome with the greatest sorrow we act not like men or women but like children whose comfort in all their troubles is to press themselves against their mother's breast, or if she be not there to hold each other tight in one another's arms.

When it was dark he brought her in with infinite precautions, yet not without the dogs scenting her, after which nothing could moderate their clamour.

Having got her into the house, the next thing he thought of was to hide her from the servants. He carried her to the bedroom in his arms and then went downstairs again.

Mr. Tebrick had three servants living in the house, the cook, the parlourmaid, and an old woman who had been his wife's nurse. Besides these women there was a groom or a gardener (whichever you choose to call him), who was a single man and so lived out, lodging with a labouring family about half a mile away.

Mr. Tebrick going downstairs pitched upon the parlourmaid.

'Janet,' says he, 'Mrs. Tebrick and I have had some bad news, and Mrs. Tebrick was called away instantly to London and left this afternoon, and I am staying to-night to put our affairs in order. We are shutting up the house, and I must give you and Mrs. Brant a month's wages and ask you to leave tomorrow morning at seven o'clock. We shall probably go away to the Continent, and I do not know when we shall come back. Please tell the others, and now get me my tea and bring it into my study on a tray.'

Janet said nothing for she was a shy girl, particularly before gentlemen, but when she entered the kitchen Mr. Tebrick heard a sudden burst of conversation with many exclamations from the cook.

When she came back with his tea, Mr. Tebrick said: 'I shall not require you upstairs. Pack your own things and tell James to have the waggonette ready for you by seven o'clock tomorrow morning to take you to the station. I am busy now, but I will see you again before you go.'

When she had gone Mr. Tebrick took the tray upstairs. For the first moment he thought the room was empty, and his vixen got away, for he could see no sign of her anywhere. But after a moment he saw something stirring in a corner of the room, and then behold! she came forth dragging her dressing-gown, into which she had somehow struggled.

This must surely have been a comical sight, but poor Mr. Tebrick was altogether too distressed then or at any time afterwards to divert himself at such ludicrous scenes. He only called to her softly:

'Silvia – Silvia. What do you do there?' And then in a moment saw for himself what she would be at, and began once more to blame himself heartily – because he had not guessed that his wife would not like to go naked, no notwithstanding the shape she was in. Nothing would satisfy him then till he had clothed her suitably, bringing her dresses from the wardrobe for her to choose. But as might have been expected, they were too big for her now, but at last he picked out a little dressing-jacket that she was fond of wearing sometimes in the mornings. It was made of a flowered silk, trimmed with lace, and the sleeves short enough to sit very well on her now. While he tied the ribands his poor lady thanked him with gentle looks and not without some

78

modesty and confusion. He propped her up in an armchair with some cushions, and they took tea together, she very delicately drinking from a saucer and taking bread and butter from his hands. All this showed him, or so he thought, that his wife was still herself; there was so little wildness in her demeanour and so much delicacy and decency, especially in her not wishing to run naked, that he was very much comforted, and began to fancy they could be happy enough if they could escape the world and live always alone.

From this too sanguine dream he was aroused by hearing the gardener speaking to the dogs, trying to quiet them, for ever since he had come in with his vixen they had been whining, barking and growling, and all as he knew because there was a fox within doors and they would kill it.

He started up now, calling to the gardener that he would come down to the dogs himself to quiet them, and bade the man go indoors again and leave it to him. All this he said in a dry, compelling kind of voice which made the fellow do as he was bid, though it was against his will, for he was curious. Mr. Tebrick went downstairs, and taking his gun from the rack loaded it and went out into the yard. Now there were two dogs, one a handsome Irish setter that was his wife's dog (she had brought it with her from Tangley Hall on her marriage); the other was an old fox terrier called Nelly that he had had ten years or more.

When he came out into the yard both dogs saluted him by barking and whining twice as much as they did before, the setter jumping up and down at the end of his chain in a frenzy, and Nelly shivering, wagging her tail, and looking first at her master and then at the house door, where she could smell the fox right enough.

There was a bright moon, so that Mr. Tebrick could see the dogs as clearly as could be. First he shot his wife's setter dead, and then looked about him for Nelly to give her the other barrel, but he could see her nowhere. The bitch was clean gone, till, looking to see how she had broken her chain, he found her lying hid in the back of her kennel. But that trick did not save her, for Mr. Tebrick, after trying to pull her out by her chain and finding it useless – she would not come, – thrust the muzzle of his gun into the kennel, pressed it into her body and so shot her. Afterwards, striking a match, he looked in at her to make certain she was dead. Then, leaving the dogs as they were, chained up, Mr. Tebrick went indoors again and found the gardener, who had not yet gone home, gave him a month's wages in lieu of notice and told him he had a job for him yet – to bury the two dogs and that he should do it that same night.

But by all this going on with so much strangeness and authority on his part, as it seemed to them, the servants were much troubled. Hearing the shots while he was out in the yard his wife's old nurse, or Nanny, ran up to the bedroom though she had no business there, and so opening the door saw the poor fox dressed in my lady's little jacket lying back in the cushions, and in such a reverie of woe that she heard nothing.

Old Nanny, though she was not expecting to find her mistress there, having been told that she was gone that afternoon to London, knew her instantly and cried out:

'Oh, my poor precious! Oh, poor Miss Silvia! What

dreadful change is this?' Then, seeing her mistress start and look at her, she cried out:

'But never fear, my darling, it will all come right, your old Nanny knows you, it will all come right in the end.'

But though she said this she did not care to look again, and kept her eyes turned away so as not to meet the foxy slit ones of her mistress, for that was too much for her. So she hurried out soon, fearing to be found there by Mr. Tebrick, and who knows, perhaps shot, like the dogs, for knowing the secret.

Mr. Tebrick had all this time gone about paying off his servants and shooting his dogs as if he were in a dream. Now he fortified himself with two or three glasses of strong whisky and went to bed, taking his vixen into his arms, where he slept soundly. Whether she did or not is more than I or anybody else can say.

In the morning when he woke up they had the place to themselves, for on his instructions the servants had all left first thing: Janet and the cook to Oxford, where they would try and find new places, and Nanny going back to the cottage near Tangley, where her son lived, who was the pigman there.

So with that morning there began what was now to be their ordinary life together. He would get up when it was broad day, and first thing light the fire downstairs and cook the breakfast, then brush his wife, sponge her with a damp sponge, then brush her again, in all this using scent very freely to hide somewhat her rank odour. When she was dressed he carried her downstairs and they had their breakfast together, she sitting up to table with him, drinking her saucer of tea, and taking her food from his fingers, or at any rate being fed by him. She was still fond of the same food that she had been used to before her transformation, a lightly boiled egg or slice of ham, a piece of buttered toast or two, with a little quince and apple jam. While I am on the subject of her food, I should say that reading in the encyclopedia he found that foxes on the Continent are inordinately fond of grapes, and that during the autumn season they abandon their ordinary diet for them, and then grow exceedingly fat and lose their offensive odour.

This appetite for grapes is so well confirmed by Æsop, and by passages in the Scriptures, that it is strange Mr. Tebrick should not have known it. After reading this account he wrote to London for a basket of grapes to be posted to him twice a week and was rejoiced to find that the account in the encyclopedia was true in the most important of these particulars. His vixen relished them exceedingly and seemed never to tire of them, so that he increased his order first from one pound to three pounds and afterwards to five. Her odour abated so much by this means that he came not to notice it at all except sometimes in the mornings before her toilet.

What helped most to make living with her bearable for him was that she understood him perfectly – yes, every word he said, and though she was dumb she expressed herself very fluently by looks and signs though never by the voice.

Thus he frequently conversed with her, telling her all his thoughts and hiding nothing from her, and this the more readily because he was very quick to catch her meaning and her answers.

'Puss, Puss,' he would say to her, for calling her that had been a habit with him always. 'Sweet Puss, some men would pity me living alone here with you after what has happened, but I would not change places while you were living with any man for the whole world. Though you are a fox I would rather live with you than any woman. I swear I would, and that too if you were changed to anything.' But then, catching her grave look, he would say: 'Do you think I jest on these things, my dear? I do not. I swear to you, my darling, that all my life I will be true to you, will be faithful, will respect and reverence you who are my wife. And I will do that not because of any hope that God in His mercy will see fit to restore your shape, but solely because I love you. However you may be changed, my love is not.'

Then anyone seeing them would have sworn that they were lovers, so passionately did each look on the other.

Often he would swear to her that the devil might have power to work some miracles, but that he would find it beyond him to change his love for her.

These passionate speeches, however they might have struck his wife in an ordinary way, now seemed to be her chief comfort. She would come to him, put her paw in his hand and look at him with sparkling eyes shining with joy and gratitude, would pant with eagerness, jump at him and lick his face.

Now he had many little things which busied him in the house – getting his meals, setting the room straight, making the bed and so forth. When he was doing this housework it was comical to watch his vixen. Often she was as it were beside herself with vexation and distress to see him in his clumsy way doing what she could have done so much better had she been able. Then, forgetful of the decency and the decorum which she had at first imposed upon herself never to run upon all fours, she followed him everywhere, and if he did one thing wrong she stopped him and showed him the way of it. When he had forgot the hour for his meal she would come and tug his sleeve and tell him as if she spoke: 'Husband, are we to have no luncheon to-day?'

This womanliness in her never failed to delight him, for it showed she was still his wife, buried as it were in the carcase of a beast but with a woman's soul. This encouraged him so much that he debated with himself whether he should not read aloud to her, as he often had done formerly. At last, since he could find no reason against it, he went to the shelf and fetched down a volume of the 'History of Clarissa Harlowe,' which he had begun to read aloud to her a few weeks before. He opened the volume where he had left off, with Lovelace's letter after he had spent the night waiting fruitlessly in the copse.

'*Good God!*

What is now to become of me?

My feet benumbed by midnight wanderings through the heaviest dews that ever fell; my wig and my linen dripping with the hoarfrost dissolving on them!

Day but just breaking . . .' etc.

While he read he was conscious of holding her attention, then after a few pages the story claimed all his, so that he read on for about half-an-hour without looking at her. When he did so he saw that she was not listening to him, but was watching something with strange eagerness. Such a fixed intent look was on her face that he was alarmed and sought the cause of it. Presently he found that her gaze was fixed on the movements of her pet dove which was in its cage hanging in the window. He spoke to her, but she seemed displeased, so he laid 'Clarissa Harlowe' aside. Nor did he ever repeat the experiment of reading to her.

Yet that same evening, as he happened to be looking through his writing table drawer with Puss beside him looking over his elbow, she spied a pack of cards, and then he was forced to pick them out to please her, then draw them from their case. At last, trying first one thing, then another, he found that what she was after was to play piquet with him. They had some difficulty at first in contriving for her to hold her cards and then to play them, but this was at last overcome by his stacking them for her on a sloping board, after which she could flip them out very neatly with her claws as she wanted to play them. When they had overcome this trouble they played three games, and most heartily she seemed to enjoy them. Moreover she won all three of them. After this they often played a quiet game of piquet together, and cribbage too. I should say that in marking the points at cribbage on the board he always moved her pegs for her as well as his own, for she could not handle them or set them in the holes.

The weather, which had been damp and misty, with frequent downpours of rain, improved very much in the following week, and, as often happens in January, there were several days with the sun shining, no wind and light frosts at night, these frosts becoming more intense as the days went on till bye and bye they began to think of snow.

With this spell of fine weather it was but natural that Mr. Tebrick should think of taking his vixen out of doors. This was something he had not yet done, both because of the damp rainy weather up till then and because the mere notion of taking her out filled him with alarm. Indeed he had so many apprehensions beforehand that at one time he resolved totally against it. For his mind was filled not only with the fear that she might escape from him and run away, which he knew was groundless, but with more rational visions, such as wandering curs, traps, gins, spring guns, besides a dread of being seen with her by the neighbourhood. At last however he resolved on it, and all the more as his vixen kept asking him in the gentlest way: 'Might she not go out into the garden?' Yet she always listened very submissively when he told her that he was afraid if they were seen together it would excite the curiosity of their neighbours; besides this, he often told her of his fears for her on account of dogs. But one day she answered this by leading him into the hall and pointing boldly to his gun. After this he resolved to take her, though with full precautions. That is he left the house door open so that in case of need she could beat a swift retreat, then he took his gun under his arm, and lastly he had her well wrapped up in a little fur jacket lest she should take cold.

He would have carried her too, but that she delicately disengaged herself from his arms and looked at him very expressively to say that she would go by herself. For already her first horror of being seen to go upon all fours was worn off; reasoning no doubt upon it, that either she must resign herself to go that way or else stay bedridden all the rest of her life.

Her joy at going into the garden was inexpressible. First she ran this way, then that, though keeping always close to him, looking very sharply with ears cocked forward first at one thing, then another and then up to catch his eye.

For some time indeed she was almost dancing with delight, running round him, then forward a yard or two, then back to him and gambolling beside him as they went round the garden. But in spite of her joy she was full of fear. At every noise, a cow lowing, a cock crowing, or a ploughman in the distance hulloaing to scare the rooks, she started, her ears pricked to catch the sound, her muzzle wrinkled up and her nose twitched, and she would then press herself against his legs. They walked round the garden and down to the pond where there were ornamental waterfowl, teal, widgeon and mandarin ducks, and seeing these again gave her great pleasure. They had always been her favourites, and now she was so overjoyed to see them that she behaved with very little of her usual self-restraint. First she stared at them, then bouncing up to her husband's knee sought to kindle an equal excitement in his mind. Whilst she rested her paws on his knee she turned her head again and again towards the ducks as though she could not take her eyes off them, and then ran down before him to the water's edge.

But her appearance threw the ducks into the utmost degree of consternation. Those on shore or near the bank swam or flew to the centre of the pond, and there huddled in a bunch; and then, swimming round and round, they began such a quacking that Mr. Tebrick was nearly deafened. As I have before said, nothing in the ludicrous way that arose out of the metamorphosis of his wife (and such incidents were plentiful) ever stood a chance of being smiled at by him. So in this case, too, for realising that the silly ducks thought his wife a fox indeed and were alarmed on that account he found painful that spectacle which to others might have been amusing.

Not so his vixen, who appeared if anything more pleased than ever when she saw in what a commotion she had set them, and began cutting a thousand pretty capers. Though at first he called to her to come back and walk another way, Mr. Tebrick was overborne by her pleasure and sat down, while

she frisked around him happier far than he had seen her ever since the change. First she ran up to him in a laughing way, all smiles, and then ran down again to the water's edge and began frisking and frolicking, chasing her own brush, dancing on her hind legs even, and rolling on the ground, then fell to running in circles, but all this without paying any heed to the ducks.

But they, with their necks craned out all pointing one way, swam to and fro in the middle of the pond, never stopping their quack, quack quack, and keeping time too, for they all quacked in chorus. Presently she came further away from the pond, and he, thinking they had had enough of this sort of entertainment, laid hold of her and said to her:

'Come, Silvia, my dear, it is growing cold, and it is time we went indoors. I am sure taking the air has done you a world of good, but we must not linger any more.'

She appeared then to agree with him, though she threw half a glance over her shoulder at the ducks, and they both walked soberly enough towards the house.

When they had gone about halfway she suddenly slipped round and was off. He turned quickly and saw the ducks had been following them.

So she drove them before her back into the pond, the ducks running in terror from her with their wings spread, and she not pressing them, for he saw that had she been so minded she could have caught two or three of the nearest. Then, with her brush waving above her, she came gambolling back to him so playfully that he stroked her indulgently, though he was first vexed, and then rather puzzled that his wife should amuse herself with such pranks.

But when they got within doors he picked her up in his arms, kissed her and spoke to her.

'Silvia, what a light-hearted childish creature you are. Your courage under misfortune shall be a lesson to me, but I cannot, I cannot bear to see it.'

Here the tears stood suddenly in his eyes, and he lay down upon the ottoman and wept, paying no heed to her until presently he was aroused by her licking his cheek and his ear.

After tea she led him to the drawing room and scratched at the door till he opened it, for this was part of the house which he had shut up, thinking three or four rooms enough for them now, and to save the dusting of it. Then it seemed she would have him play to her on the pianoforte: she led him to it, nay, what is more, she would herself pick out the music he was to play. First it was a fugue of Handel's, then one of Mendelssohn's Songs Without Words, and then 'The Diver,' and then music from Gilbert and Sullivan; but each piece of music she picked out was gayer than the last one. Thus they sat happily engrossed for perhaps an hour in the candle light until the extreme cold in that unwarmed room stopped his playing and drove them downstairs to the fire. Thus did she admirably comfort her husband when he was dispirited.

Yet next morning when he woke he was distressed when he found that she was not in the bed with him but was lying curled up at the foot of it. During breakfast she hardly listened when he spoke, and then impatiently, but sat staring at the dove.

Mr. Tebrick sat silently looking out of window for some time, then he took out his pocket book; in it there was a photograph of his wife taken soon after their wedding. Now he gazed and gazed upon those familiar features, and now he lifted his head and looked at the animal before him. He laughed then bitterly, the first and last time for that matter that Mr. Tebrick ever laughed at his wife's transformation, for he was not very humorous. But this laugh was sour and painful to him. Then he tore up the photograph into little pieces, and scattered them out of the window, saying to himself: 'Memories will not help me here,' and turning to the vixen he saw that she was still staring at the caged bird, and as he looked he saw her lick her chops.

He took the bird into the next room, then acting suddenly upon the impulse, he opened the cage door and set it free, saying as he did so:

'Go, poor bird! Fly from this wretched house while you still remember your mistress who fed you from her coral lips. You are not a fit plaything for her now. Farewell, poor bird!

88

Farewell! Unless,' he added with a melancholy smile, 'you return with good tidings like Noah's dove.'

But, poor gentleman, his troubles were not over yet, and indeed one may say that he ran to meet them by his constant supposing that his lady should still be the same to a tittle in her behaviour now that she was changed into a fox.

Without making any unwarrantable suppositions as to her soul or what had now become of it (though we could find a good deal to the purpose on that point in the system of Paracelsus), let us consider only how much the change in her body must needs affect her ordinary conduct. So that before we judge too harshly of this unfortunate lady, we must reflect upon the physical necessities and infirmities and appetites of her new condition, and we must magnify the fortitude of her mind which enabled her to behave with decorum, cleanliness and decency in spite of her new situation.

Thus she might have been expected to befoul her room, yet never could anyone, whether man or beast, have shown more nicety in such matters. But at luncheon Mr. Tebrick helped her to a wing of chicken, and leaving the room for a minute to fetch some water which he had forgot, found her at his return on the table crunching the very bones. He stood silent, dismayed and wounded to the heart at this sight. For we must observe that this unfortunate husband thought always of his vixen as that gentle and delicate woman she had lately been. So that whenever his vixen's conduct went beyond that which he expected in his wife he was, as it were, cut to the quick, and no kind of agony could be greater to him than to see her thus forget herself. On this account it may indeed be regretted that Mrs. Tebrick had been so exactly well-bred, and in particular that her table manners had always been scrupulous. Had she been in the habit, like a continental princess I have dined with, of taking her leg of chicken by the drumstick and gnawing the flesh, it had been far better for him now. But as her manners had been perfect, so the lapse of them was proportionately painful to him. Thus in this instance he stood as it were in silent agony till she had finished her hideous crunching of the chicken bones and had devoured every scrap. Then he spoke to her gently, taking her on to his knee, stroking her fur and fed her with a few grapes, saying to her:

'Silvia, Silvia, is it so hard for you? Try and remember the past, my darling, and by living with me we will quite forget that you are no longer a woman. Surely this affliction will pass soon, as suddenly as it came, and it will all seem to us like an evil dream.'

Yet though she appeared perfectly sensible of his words and gave him sorrowful and penitent looks like her old self, that same afternoon, on taking her out, he had all the difficulty in the world to keep her from going near the ducks.

There came to him then a thought that was very disagreeable to him, namely, that he dare not trust his wife alone with any bird or she would kill it. And this was the more shocking to him to think of since it meant that he durst not trust her as much as a dog even. For we may trust dogs who are familiars, with all the household pets; nay more, we can put them upon trust with anything and know they will not touch it, not even if they be starving. But things were come to such a pass with his vixen that he dared not in his heart trust her at all. Yet she was still in many ways so much more woman than fox that he could talk to her on any subject and she would understand him, better far than the oriental women who are kept in subjection can ever understand their masters unless they converse on the most trifling household topics.

Thus she understood excellently well the importance and duties of religion. She would listen with approval in the evening when he said the Lord's Prayer, and was rigid in her observance of the Sabbath. Indeed, the next day being Sunday he, thinking no harm, proposed their usual game of piquet, but no, she would not play. Mr. Tebrick, not understanding at first what she meant, though he was usually very quick with her, he proposed it to her again, which she again refused, and this time, to show her meaning, made the sign of the cross with her paw. This exceedingly rejoiced and comforted him in his distress. He begged her pardon, and fervently thanked God for having so good a wife, who, in spite of all, knew more of her duty to God than he did. But here I must warn the reader from inferring that she was a papist because she then made the sign of the cross. She made that sign to my thinking only on compulsion because she could not express herself except in that way. For she had been brought up as a true Protestant, and that she still was one is confirmed by her objection to cards, which would have been less than nothing to her had she been a papist. Yet that evening, taking her into the drawing room so that he might play her some sacred music, he found her after some time cowering away from him in the farthest corner of the room, her ears flattened back and an expression of the greatest anguish in her eyes. When he spoke to her she licked his hand, but remained shivering for a long time at his feet and showed the clearest symptoms of terror if he so much as moved towards the piano.

On seeing this and recollecting how ill the ears of a dog can bear with our music, and how this dislike might be expected to be even greater in a fox, all of whose senses are more acute from being a wild creature, recollecting this he closed the piano and taking her in his arms, locked up the room and never went into it again. He could not help marvelling though, since it was but two days after she had herself led him there, and even picked out for him to play and sing those pieces which were her favourites.

That night she would not sleep with him, neither in the bed nor on it, so that he was forced to let her curl herself up on the floor. But neither would she sleep there, for several times she woke him by trotting around the room, and once when he had got sound asleep by springing on the bed and then off it, so that he woke with a violent start and cried out, but got no answer either, except hearing her trotting round and round the room. Presently he imagines to himself that she must want something, and so fetches her food and water, but she never so much as looks at it, but still goes on her rounds, every now and then scratching at the door.

Though he spoke to her, calling her by her name, she would pay no heed to him, or else only for the moment. At last he gave her up and said to her plainly: 'The fit is on you now Silvia to be a fox, but I shall keep you close and in the morning you will recollect yourself and thank me for having kept you now.'

So he lay down again, but not to sleep, only to listen to his wife running about the room and trying to get out of it. Thus he spent what was perhaps the most miserable night of his existence. In the morning she was still restless, and was reluctant to let him wash and brush her, and appeared to dislike being scented but as it were to bear with it for his sake. Ordinarily she had taken the greatest pleasure imaginable in her toilet, so that on this account, added to his sleepless night, Mr. Tebrick was utterly dejected, and it was then that he resolved to put a project into execution that would show him, so he thought, whether he had a wife or only a wild vixen in his house. But yet he was comforted that she bore at all with him, though so restlessly that he did not spare her, calling her a 'bad wild fox.' And then speaking to her in this manner: 'Are you not ashamed, Silvia, to be such a madcap, such a wicked hoyden? You who were particular in dress. I see it was all vanity – now you have not your former advantages you think nothing of decency.'

His words had some effect with her too, and with himself, so that by the time he had finished dressing her they were both in the lowest state of spirits imaginable and neither of them far from tears.

Breakfast she took soberly enough, and after that he went about getting his experiment ready, which was this. In the garden he gathered together a nosegay of snowdrops, those being all the flowers he could find, and then going into the village of Stokoe bought a Dutch rabbit (that is a black and white one) from a man there who kept them.

When he got back he took her flowers and at the same time set down the basket with the rabbit in it, with the lid open. Then he called to her: 'Silvia, I have brought some flowers for you. Look, the first snowdrops.'

At this she ran up very prettily, and never giving as much as one glance at the rabbit which had hopped out of its basket, she began to thank him for the flowers. Indeed she seemed

indefatigable in shewing her gratitude, smelt them, stood a little way off looking at them, then thanked him again. Mr. Tebrick (and this was all part of his plan) then took a vase and went to find some water for them, but left the flowers beside her. He stopped away five minutes, timing it by his watch and listening very intently, but never heard the rabbit squeak. Yet when he went in what a horrid shambles was spread before his eyes. Blood on the carpet, blood on the armchairs and antimacassars, even a little blood spurtled on to the wall, and what was worse, Mrs. Tebrick tearing and growling over a piece of the skin and the legs, for she had eaten up all the rest of it. The poor gentleman was so heartbroken over this that he was like to have done himself an injury, and at one moment thought of getting his gun, to have shot himself and his vixen too. Indeed the extremity of his grief was such that it served him a very good turn, for he was so entirely unmanned by it that for some time he could do nothing but weep, and fell into a chair with his head in his hands, and so kept weeping and groaning.

After he had been some little while employed in this dismal way, his vixen, who had by this time bolted down the rabbit skin, head, ears and all, came to him and putting her paws on his knees, thrust her long muzzle into his face and began licking him. But he, looking at her now with different eyes, and seeing her jaws still sprinkled with fresh blood and her claws full of the rabbit's fleck, would have none of it.

But though he beat her off four or five times even to giving her blows and kicks, she still came back to him, crawling on her belly and imploring his forgiveness with wide-open sorrowful eyes. Before he had made this rash experiment of the rabbit and the flowers, he had promised himself that if she failed in it he would have no more feeling or compassion for her than if she were in truth a wild vixen out of the woods. This resolution, though the reasons for it had seemed to him so very plain before, he now found more difficult to carry out than to decide on. At length after cursing her and beating her off for upwards of half-an-hour, he admitted to himself that he still did care for her, and even loved her dearly in spite of all, whatever pretence he affected towards her. When he had acknowledged this he looked up at her and met her eyes fixed upon him, and held out his arms to her and said:

'Oh Silvia, Silvia, would you had never done this! Would I had never tempted you in a fatal hour! Does not this butchery and eating of raw meat and rabbit's fur disgust you? Are you a monster in your soul as well as in your body? Have you forgotten what it is to be a woman?'

Meanwhile, with every word of his, she crawled a step nearer on her belly and at last climbed sorrowfully into his arms. His words then seemed to take effect on her and her eyes filled with tears and she wept most penitently in his arms, and her body shook with her sobs as if her heart were breaking. This sorrow of hers gave him the strangest mixture of pain and joy that he had ever known, for his love for her returning with a rush, he could not bear to witness her pain and yet must take pleasure in it as it fed his hopes of her one day returning to be a woman. So the more anguish of shame his vixen underwent, the greater his hopes rose, till his love and pity for her increasing equally, he was almost wishing her to be nothing more than a mere fox than to suffer so much by being half-human.

At last he looked about him somewhat dazed with so much weeping, then set his vixen down on the ottoman, and began to clean up the room with a heavy heart. He fetched a pail of water and washed out all the stains of blood, gathered up the two antimacassars and fetched clean ones from the other rooms. While he went about this work his vixen sat and watched him very contritely with her nose between her two front paws, and when he had done he brought in some luncheon for himself, though it was already late, but none for her, she having lately so infamously feasted. But water he gave her and a bunch of grapes. Afterwards she led him to the small tortoiseshell cabinet and would have him open it. When he had done so she motioned to the portable stereoscope which lay inside. Mr. Tebrick instantly fell in with her wish and after a few trials adjusted it to her vision. Thus they spent the rest of the afternoon together very happily looking through the collection of views which he had purchased, of Italy, Spain and Scotland. This diversion gave her great apparent pleasure and afforded him considerable comfort. But that night he could not prevail upon her to sleep in bed with him, and finally allowed her to sleep on a mat beside the bed where he could stretch down and touch her. So they passed the night, with his hand upon her head.

The next morning he had more of a struggle than ever to wash and dress her. Indeed at one time nothing but holding her by the scruff prevented her from getting away from him,

95

but at last he achieved his object and she was washed, brushed, scented and dressed, although to be sure this left him better pleased than her, for she regarded her silk jacket with disfavour.

Still at breakfast she was well mannered though a trifle hasty with her food. Then his difficulties with her began for she would go out, but as he had his housework to do, he could not allow it. He brought her picture books to divert her, but she would have none of them but stayed at the door scratching it with her claws industriously till she had worn away the paint.

At first he tried coaxing her and wheedling, gave her cards to play patience and so on, but finding nothing would distract her from going out, his temper began to rise, and he told her plainly that she must wait his pleasure and that he had as much natural obstinacy as she had. But to all that he said she paid no heed whatever but only scratched the harder.

Thus he let her continue until luncheon, when she would not sit up, or eat off a plate, but first was for getting on to the table, and when that was prevented, snatched her meat and ate it under the table. To all his rebukes she turned a deaf or sullen ear, and so they each finished their meal eating little, either of them, for till she would sit at table he would give her no more, and his vexation had taken away his own appetite. In the afternoon he took her out for her airing in the garden.

She made no pretence now of enjoying the first snowdrops or the view from the terrace. No – there was only one thing for her now – the ducks, and she was off to them before he could stop her. Luckily they were all swimming when she got there (for a stream running into the pond on the far side it was not frozen there).

When he had got down to the pond, she ran out on to the ice, which would not bear his weight, and though he called her and begged her to come back she would not heed him but stayed frisking about, getting as near the ducks as she dared, but being circumspect in venturing on to the thin ice.

Presently she turned on herself and began tearing off her clothes, and at last by biting got off her little jacket and taking it in her mouth stuffed it into a hole in the ice where he could not get it. Then she ran hither and thither a stark naked vixen, and without giving a glance to her poor husband who stood silently now upon the bank, with despair and terror settled in his mind. She let him stay there most of the afternoon till he was chilled through and through and worn out with watching her. At last he reflected how she had just stripped herself and how in the morning she struggled against being dressed, and he thought perhaps he was too strict with her and if he let her have her own way they could manage to be happy somehow together even if she did eat off the floor. So he called out to her then:

'Silvia, come now, be good, you shan't wear any more clothes if you don't want to, and you needn't sit at table neither, I promise. You shall do as you like in that, but you must give up one thing, and that is you must stay with me and not go out alone, for that is dangerous. If any dog came on you he would kill you.'

Directly he had finished speaking she came to him joyously, began fawning on him and prancing round him so that in spite of his vexation with her, and being cold, he could not help stroking her.

'Oh, Silvia, are you not wilful and cunning? I see you glory in being so, but I shall not reproach you but shall stick to my side of the bargain, and you must stick to yours.'

He built a big fire when he came back to the house and took a glass or two of spirits also, to warm himself up, for he was chilled to the very bone. Then, after they had dined, to cheer himself he took another glass, and then another, and so on till he was very merry, he thought. Then he would play with his vixen, she encouraging him with her pretty sportiveness. He got up to catch her then and finding himself unsteady on his legs, he went down on to all fours. The long and the short of it is that by drinking he drowned all his sorrow; and then would be a beast too like his wife, though she was one through no fault of her own, and could not help it. To what lengths he went then in that drunken humour I shall not offend my readers by relating, but shall only say that he was so drunk and sottish that he had a very imperfect recollection of what had passed when he woke the next morning. There is no exception to the rule that if a man drink heavily at night the next morning will show the other side to his nature. Thus with Mr. Tebrick, for as he had been beastly, merry and a very dare-devil the night before, so on his awakening was he ashamed, melancholic and a true penitent before his Creator. The first thing he did when he came to himself was to call out to God to forgive him for his sin, then he fell into earnest prayer and continued so for half-an-hour upon his knees. Then he got up and dressed but continued very melancholy for the whole of the morning. Being in this mood you may imagine it hurt him to see his wife running about naked, but he reflected it would be a bad reformation that began with breaking faith. He had made a bargain and he would stick to it, and so he let her be, though sorely against his will.

For the same reason, that is because he would stick to his side of the bargain, he did not require her to sit up at table, but gave her her breakfast on a dish in the corner, where to tell the truth she on her side ate it all up with great daintiness and propriety. Nor she did make any attempt to go out of doors that morning, but lay curled up in an armchair before the fire dozing. After lunch he took her out, and she never so much as offered to go near the ducks, but running before him led him on to take her a longer walk. This he consented to do very much to her joy and delight. He took her through the fields by the most unfrequented ways, being much alarmed lest they should be seen by anyone. But by good luck they walked above four miles across country and saw nobody. All the way his wife kept running on ahead of him, and then back to him to lick his hand and so on, and appeared delighted at taking exercise. And though they started two or three rabbits and a hare in the course of their walk she never attempted to go after them, only giving them a look and then looking back to him, laughing at him as it were for his warning cry of 'Puss! come in, no nonsense now!'

Just when they got home and were going into the porch

they came face to face with an old woman. Mr. Tebrick stopped short in consternation and looked about for his vixen, but she had run forward without any shyness to greet her. Then he recognised the intruder, it was his wife's old nurse.

'What are you doing here, Mrs. Cork?' he asked her.

Mrs. Cork answered him in these words:

'Poor thing. Poor Miss Silvia! It is a shame to let her run about like a dog. It is a shame, and your own wife too. But whatever she looks like, you should trust her the same as ever. If you do she'll do her best to be a good wife to you, if you don't I shouldn't wonder if she did turn into a proper fox. I saw her, sir, before I left, and I've had no peace of mind. I couldn't sleep thinking of her. So I've come back to look after her, as I have done all her life, sir,' and she stooped down and took Mrs. Tebrick by the paw.

Mr. Tebrick unlocked the door and they went in. When Mrs. Cork saw the house she exclaimed again and again: 'The place was a pigstye. They couldn't live like that, a gentleman must have somebody to look after him. She would do it. He could trust her with the secret.'

Had the old woman come the day before it is likely enough that Mr. Tebrick would have sent her packing. But the voice of conscience being woken in him by his drunkenness of the night before he was heartily ashamed of his own management of the business, moreover the old woman's words that 'it was a shame to let her run about like a dog,' moved him exceedingly. Being in this mood the truth is he welcomed her.

But we may conclude that Mrs. Tebrick was as sorry to see her old Nanny as her husband was glad. If we consider that she had been brought up strictly by her when she was a child, and was now again in her power, and that her old nurse could never be satisfied with her now whatever she did, but would always think her wicked to be a fox at all, there seems good reason for her dislike. And it is possible, too, that there may have been another cause as well, and that is jealousy. We know her husband was always trying to bring her back to be a woman, or at any rate to get her to act like one, may she not have been hoping to get him to be like a beast himself or to act like one? May she not have thought it easier to change him thus than ever to change herself back into being a woman? If we think that she had had a success of this kind only the night before, when he got drunk, can we not conclude that this was indeed the case, and then we have another good reason why the poor lady should hate to see her old nurse?

It is certain that whatever hopes Mr. Tebrick had of Mrs. Cork affecting his wife for the better were disappointed. She grew steadily wilder and after a few days so intractable with her that Mr. Tebrick again took her under his complete control.

The first morning Mrs. Cork made her a new jacket, cutting down the sleeves of a blue silk one of Mrs. Tebrick's and trimming it with swan's down, and directly she had altered it, put it on her mistress, and fetching a mirror would have her admire the fit of it. All the time she waited on Mrs. Tebrick the old woman talked to her as though she were a baby, and treated her as such, never thinking perhaps that she was either the one thing or the other, that is either a lady to whom she owed respect and who had rational powers exceeding her own, or else a wild creature on whom words were wasted. But though at first she submitted passively, Mrs. Tebrick only waited for her Nanny's back to be turned to tear up her pretty piece of handiwork into shreds, and then ran gaily about waving her brush with only a few ribands still hanging from her neck.

So it was time after time (for the old woman was used to having her own way) until Mrs. Cork would, I think, have tried punishing her if she had not been afraid of Mrs. Tebrick's rows of white teeth, which she often showed her, then laughing afterwards, as if to say it was only play.

Not content with tearing off the dresses that were fitted on her, one day Silvia slipped upstairs to her wardrobe and tore down all her old dresses and made havoc with them, not sparing her wedding dress either, but tearing and ripping them all up so that there was hardly a shred or rag left big enough to dress a doll in. On this, Mr. Tebrick, who had let the old woman have most of her management to see what she could make of her, took her back under his own control.

He was sorry enough now that Mrs. Cork had disappointed him in the hopes he had had of her, to have the old woman, as it were, on his hands. True she could be useful enough in many ways to him, by doing the housework, the cooking and mending, but still he was anxious since his secret was in her keeping, and the more now that she had tried her hand with his wife and failed. For he saw that vanity had kept her mouth shut if she had won over her mistress to better ways, and her love for her would have grown by getting her own way with her. But now that she had failed she bore her mistress a grudge for not being won over, or at the best was become indifferent to the business, so that she might very readily blab.

For the moment all Mr. Tebrick could do was to keep her from going into Stokoe to the village, where she would meet all her old cronies and where there were certain to be any number of inquiries about what was going on at Rylands and so on. But as he saw that it was clearly beyond his power, however vigilant he might be, to watch over the old woman and his wife, and to prevent anyone from meeting with either of them, he began to consider what he could best do.

Since he had sent away his servants and the gardener, giving out a story of having received bad news and his wife going away to London where he would join her, their probably going out of England and so on, he knew well enough that there would be a great deal of talk in the neighbourhood.

And as he had now stayed on, contrary to what he had said, there would be further rumour. Indeed, had he known it, there was a story already going round the country that his wife had run away with Major Solmes, and that he was gone mad with grief, that he had shot his dogs and his horses and shut himself up alone in the house and would speak with no one. This story was made up by his neighbours not because they were fanciful or wanted to deceive, but like most tittle-tattle to fill a gap, as few like to confess ignorance, and if people are asked about such or such a man they must have something to say, or they suffer in everybody's opinion, are set down as dull or 'out of the swim.' In this way I met not long ago with someone who, after talking some little while and not knowing me or who I was, told me that David Garnett was dead, and died of being bitten by a cat after he had tormented it. He had long grown a nuisance to his friends as an exorbitant sponge upon them, and the world was well rid of him.

Hearing this story of myself diverted me at the time, but I fully believe it has served me in good stead since. For it set me on my guard as perhaps nothing else would have done, against accepting for true all floating rumour and village gossip, so that now I am by second nature a true sceptic and scarcely believe anything unless the evidence for it is conclusive. Indeed I could never have got to the bottom of this history if I had believed one tenth part of what I was told, there was so much of it that was either manifestly false and absurd, or else contradictory to the ascertained facts. It is therefore only the bare bones of the story which you will find written here, for I have rejected all the flowery embroideries which would be entertaining reading enough, I daresay, for some, but if there be any doubt of the truth of a thing it is poor sort of entertainment to read about in my opinion.

To get back to our story: Mr. Tebrick having considered how much the appetite of his neighbours would be whetted to find out the mystery by his remaining in that part of the country, determined that the best thing he could do was to remove.

After some time turning the thing over in his mind, he decided that no place would be so good for his purpose as old Nanny's cottage. It was thirty miles away from Stokoe, which in the country means as far as Timbuctoo does to us in London. Then it was near Tangley, and his lady having known it from her childhood would feel at home there, and also it was utterly remote, there being no village near it or manor house other than Tangley Hall, which was now untenanted for the greater part of the year. Nor did it mean imparting his secret to others, for there was only Mrs. Cork's son, a widower, who being out at work all day would be easily outwitted, the more so as he was stone deaf and of a slow and saturnine disposition. To be sure there was little Polly, Mrs. Cork's granddaughter, but either Mr. Tebrick forgot her altogether, or else reckoned her as a mere baby and not to be thought of as a danger.

He talked the thing over with Mrs. Cork, and they decided upon it out of hand. The truth is the old woman was beginning to regret that her love and her curiosity had ever brought her back to Rylands, since so far she had got much work and little credit by it.

When it was settled, Mr. Tebrick disposed of the remaining business he had at Rylands in the afternoon, and that was chiefly putting out his wife's riding horse into the keeping of a farmer near by, for he thought he would drive over with his own horse, and the other spare horse tandem in the dogcart.

The next morning they locked up the house and they departed, having first secured Mrs. Tebrick in a large wicker hamper where she would be tolerably comfortable. This was for safety, for in the agitation of driving she might jump out, and on the other hand, if a dog scented her and she were loose, she might be in danger of her life. Mr. Tebrick drove with the hamper beside him on the front seat, and spoke to her gently very often.

She was overcome by the excitement of the journey and kept poking her nose first through one crevice, then through another, turning and twisting the whole time and peeping out to see what they were passing. It was a bitterly cold day, and when they had gone about fifteen miles they drew up by the roadside to rest the horses and have their own luncheon, for he dared not stop at an inn. He knew that any living creature in a hamper, even if it be only an old fowl, always draws attention; there would be several loafers most likely who would notice that he had a fox with him, and even if he left the hamper in the cart the dogs at the inn would be sure to sniff out her scent. So not to take any chances he drew up at

103

the side of the road and rested there, though it was freezing hard and a north-east wind howling.

He took down his precious hamper, unharnessed his two horses, covered them with rugs and gave them their corn. Then he opened the basket and let his wife out. She was quite beside herself with joy, running hither and thither, bouncing up on him, looking about her and even rolling over on the ground. Mr. Tebrick took this to mean that she was glad at making this journey and rejoiced equally with her. As for Mrs. Cork, she sat motionless on the back seat of the dogcart well wrapped up, eating her sandwiches, but would not speak a word. When they had stayed there half-an-hour Mr. Tebrick harnessed the horses again, though he was so cold he could scarcely buckle the straps, and put his vixen in her basket, but seeing that she wanted to look about her, he let her tear away the osiers with her teeth till she had made a hole big enough for her to put her head out of.

They drove on again and then the snow began to come down and that in earnest, so that he began to be afraid they would never cover the ground. But just after nightfall they got in, and he was content to leave unharnessing the horses and baiting them to Simon, Mrs. Cork's son. His vixen was tired by then, as well as he, and they slept together, he in the bed and she under it, very contentedly.

The next morning he looked about him at the place and found the thing there that he most wanted, and that was a little walled-in garden where his wife could run in freedom and yet be in safety.

After they had had breakfast she was wild to go out into the snow. So they went out together, and he had never seen such a mad creature in all his life as his wife was then. For she ran to and fro as if she were crazy, biting at the snow and rolling in it, and round and round in circles and rushed back at him fiercely as if she meant to bite him. He joined her in the frolic, and began snowballing her till she was so wild that it was all he could do to quiet her again and bring her indoors for luncheon. Indeed with her gambollings she tracked the whole garden over with her feet; he could see where she had rolled in the snow and where she had danced in it, and looking at those prints of her feet as they went in, made his heart ache, he knew not why.

They passed the first day at old Nanny's cottage happily enough, without their usual bickerings, and this because of the novelty of the snow which had diverted them. In the afternoon he first showed his wife to little Polly, who eyed her very curiously but hung back shyly and seemed a good deal afraid of the fox. But Mr. Tebrick took up a book and let them get acquainted by themselves, and presently looking up saw that they had come together and Polly was stroking his wife, patting her and running her fingers through her fur. Presently she began talking to the fox, and then brought her doll in to show her so that very soon they were very good playmates together. Watching the two gave Mr. Tebrick great delight, and in particular when he noticed that there was something very motherly in his vixen. She was indeed far above the child in intelligence and restrained herself too from any hasty action. But while she seemed to wait on Polly's pleasure yet she managed to give a twist to the game whatever it was, that never failed to delight the little girl. In short, in a very little while, Polly was so taken with her new playmate that she cried when she was parted from her and wanted her always with her. This disposition of Mrs. Tebrick's made Mrs. Cork more agreeable than she had been lately either to the husband or the wife.

Three days after they had come to the cottage the weather changed, and they woke up one morning to find the snow gone, and the wind in the south, and the sun shining, so that it was like the first beginning of spring.

Mr. Tebrick let his vixen out into the garden after breakfast, stayed with her awhile, and then went indoors to write some letters.

When he got out again he could see no sign of her anywhere, so that he ran about bewildered, calling to her. At last he spied a mound of fresh earth by the wall in one corner of the garden, and running thither found that there was a hole freshly dug seeming to go under the wall. On this he ran out of the garden quickly till he came to the other side of the wall, but there was no hole there, so he concluded that she was not yet got through. So it proved to be, for reaching down into the hole he felt her brush with his hand, and could hear her distinctly working away with her claws. He called to her then, saying: 'Silvia, Silvia, why do you do this? Are you trying to escape from me? I am your husband, and if I keep you confined it is to protect you, not to let you run into danger. Show me how I can make you happy and I will do it, but do not try to escape from me. I love you, Silvia; is it because of that that you want to fly from me to go into the world where you will be in danger of your life always? There are dogs everywhere and they all would kill you if it were not for me. Come out, Silvia, come out.'

But Silvia would not listen to him, so he waited there silent. Then he spoke to her in a different way, asking her had she forgot the bargain she made with him that she would not go out alone, but now when she had all the liberty of a garden to

herself would she wantonly break her word? And he asked her, were they not married? And had she not always found him a good husband to her? But she heeded this neither until presently his temper getting somewhat out of hand he cursed her obstinacy and told her if she would be a damned fox she was welcome to it, for his part he could get his own way. She had not escaped yet. He would dig her out for he still had time, and if she struggled put her in a bag.

These words brought her forth instantly and she looked at him with as much astonishment as if she knew not what could have made him angry. Yes, she even fawned on him, but in a good-natured kind of way, as if she were a very good wife putting up wonderfully with her husband's temper.

These airs of hers made the poor gentleman (so simple was he) repent his outburst and feel most ashamed.

But for all that when she was out of the hole he filled it up with great stones and beat them in with a crowbar so she should find her work at that point harder than before if she was tempted to begin it again.

In the afternoon he let her go again into the garden but sent little Polly with her to keep her company. But presently on looking out he saw his vixen had climbed up into the limbs of an old pear tree and was looking over the wall, and was not so far from it but she might jump over it if she could get a little further.

Mr. Tebrick ran out into the garden as quick as he could, and when his wife saw him it seemed she was startled and made a false spring at the wall, so that she missed reaching it and fell back heavily to the ground and lay there insensible. When Mr. Tebrick got up to her he found her head was twisted under her by her fall and the neck seemed to be broken. The shock was so great to him that for some time he could not do anything, but knelt beside her turning her limp body stupidly in his hands. At length he recognised that she was indeed dead, and beginning to consider what dreadful afflictions God had visited him with, he blasphemed horribly and called on God to strike him dead, or give his wife back to him.

'Is it not enough,' he cried, adding a foul blasphemous oath, 'that you should rob me of my dear wife, making her a fox, but now you must rob me of that fox too, that has been my only solace and comfort in this affliction?'

Then he burst into tears and began wringing his hands and continued there in such an extremity of grief for half-an-hour that he cared nothing, neither what he was doing, nor what would become of him in the future, but only knew that his life was ended now and he would not live any longer than he could help.

All this while the little girl Polly stood by, first staring, then asking him what had happened, and lastly crying with fear, but he never heeded her nor looked at her but only tore his hair, sometimes shouted at God, or shook his fist at Heaven. So in a fright Polly opened the door and ran out of the garden.

At length worn out, and as it were all numb with his loss, Mr. Tebrick got up and went within doors, leaving his dear fox lying near where she had fallen.

He stayed indoors only two minutes and then came out again with a razor in his hand intending to cut his own throat, for he was out of his senses in this first paroxysm of grief.

But his vixen was gone, at which he looked about for a moment bewildered, and then enraged, thinking that somebody must have taken the body.

The door of the garden being open he ran straight through it. Now this door, which had been left ajar by Polly when she ran off, opened into a little courtyard where the fowls were shut in at night; the woodhouse and the privy also stood there. On the far side of it from the garden gate were two large wooden doors big enough when open to let a cart enter, and high enough to keep a man from looking over into the yard.

When Mr. Tebrick got into the yard he found his vixen leaping up at these doors, and wild with terror, but as lively as ever he saw her in his life. He ran up to her but she shrank away from him, and would then have dodged him too, but he caught hold of her. She bared her teeth at him but he paid no heed to that, only picked her straight up into his arms and took her so indoors. Yet all the while he could scarce believe his eyes to see her living, and felt her all over very carefully to find if she had not some bones broken. But no, he could find none. Indeed it was some hours before this poor silly gentleman began to suspect the truth, which was that his vixen had practised a deception upon him, and all the time he was bemoaning his loss in such heartrending terms, she was only shamming death to run away directly she was able. If it had not been that the yard gates were shut, which was a mere chance, she had got her liberty by that trick. And that this was only a trick of hers to sham dead was plain when he had thought it over. Indeed it is an old and time-honoured trick of the fox. It is in Æsop and a hundred other writers have confirmed it since. But so thoroughly had he been deceived by her, that at first he was as much overcome with joy at his wife still being alive, as he had been with grief a little while before, thinking her dead.

He took her in his arms, hugging her to him and thanking God a dozen times for her preservation. But his kissing and fondling her had very little effect now, for she did not answer him by licking or soft looks, but stayed huddled up and sullen, with her hair bristling on her neck and her ears laid back every time he touched her. At first he thought this might be because he had touched some broken bone or tender place where she had been hurt, but at last the truth came to him.

Thus he was again to suffer, and though the pain of knowing her treachery to him was nothing to the grief of losing her, yet it was more insidious and lasting. At first, from a mere nothing, this pain grew gradually until it was a torture to him. If he had been one of your stock ordinary husbands, such a one who by experience has learnt never to enquire too closely into his wife's doings, her comings or goings, and never to ask her, 'How she has spent the day?' for fear he should be made the more of a fool, had Mr. Tebrick been such a one he had been luckier, and his pain would have been almost nothing. But you must consider that he had never been deceived once by his wife in the course of their married life. No, she had never told him as much as one white lie, but had always been frank, open and ingenuous as if she and her husband were not husband and wife, or indeed of opposite sexes. Yet we must rate him as very foolish, that living thus with a fox, which beast has the same reputation for deceitfulness, craft and cunning, in all countries, all ages, and amongst all races of mankind, he should expect this fox to be as candid and honest with him in all things as the country girl he had married.

His wife's sullenness and bad temper continued that day, for she cowered away from him and hid under the sofa, nor could he persuade her to come out from there. Even when it was her dinner time she stayed, refusing resolutely to be tempted out with food, and lying so quiet that he heard nothing from her for hours. At night he carried her up to the bedroom, but she was still sullen and refused to eat a morsel, though she drank a little water during the night, when she fancied he was asleep.

The next morning was the same, and by now Mr. Tebrick had been through all the agonies of wounded self-esteem, disillusionment and despair that a man can suffer. But though his emotions rose up in his heart and nearly stifled him he showed no sign of them to her, neither did he abate one jot his tenderness and consideration for his vixen. At breakfast he tempted her with a freshly killed young pullet. It hurt him to make this advance to her, for hitherto he had kept her strictly on cooked meats, but the pain of seeing her refuse it was harder still for him to bear. Added to this was now an anxiety lest she should starve herself to death rather than stay with him any longer.

All that morning he kept her close, but in the afternoon let her loose again in the garden after he had lopped the pear tree so that she could not repeat her performance of climbing.

But seeing how disgustedly she looked while he was by, never offering to run or to play as she was used, but only standing stock still with her tail between her legs, her ears flattened, and the hair bristling on her shoulders, seeing this he left her to herself out of mere humanity.

When he came out after half-an-hour he found that she was gone, but there was a fair sized hole by the wall, and she just buried all but her brush, digging desperately to get under the wall and make her escape.

He ran up to the hole, and put his arm in after her and called to her to come out, but she would not. So at first he began pulling her out by the shoulder, then his hold slipping, by the hind legs. As soon as he had drawn her forth she whipped round and snapped at his hand and bit it through near the joint of the thumb, but let it go instantly.

They stayed there for a minute facing each other, he on his knees and she facing him the picture of unrepentant wickedness and fury. Being thus on his knees, Mr. Tebrick was down on her level very nearly, and her muzzle was thrust almost into his face. Her ears lay flat on her head, her gums were bared in a silent snarl, and all her beautiful teeth threatening him that she would bite him again. Her back too was half-arched, all her hair bristling and her brush held drooping. But it was her eyes that held his, with their slit pupils looking at him with savage desperation and rage.

The blood ran very freely from his hand but he never noticed that or the pain of it either, for all his thoughts were for his wife.

'What is this, Silvia?' he said very quietly, 'what is this? Why are you so savage now? If I stand between you and your freedom it is because I love you. Is it such torment to be with me?' But Silvia never stirred a muscle.

'You would not do this if you were not in anguish, poor beast, you want your freedom. I cannot keep you, I cannot hold you to vows made when you were a woman. Why, you have forgotten who I am.'

The tears then began running down his cheeks, he sobbed, and said to her:

'Go – I shall not keep you. Poor beast, poor beast, I love you, I love you. Go if you want to. But if you remember me come back. I shall never keep you against your will. Go – go. But kiss me now.'

He leant forward then and put his lips to her snarling fangs, but though she kept snarling she did not bite him. Then he got up quickly and went to the door of the garden that opened into a little paddock against a wood.

When he opened it she went through it like an arrow, crossed the paddock like a puff of smoke and in a moment was gone from his sight. Then, suddenly finding himself alone, Mr. Tebrick came as it were to himself and ran after her, calling her by name and shouting to her, and so went plunging into the wood, and through it for about a mile, running almost blindly.

At last when he was worn out he sat down, seeing that she had gone beyond recovery and it was already night. Then, rising, he walked slowly homewards, wearied and spent in spirit. As he went he bound up his hand that was still running with blood. His coat was torn, his hat lost, and his face scratched right across with briars. Now in cold blood he began to reflect on what he had done and to repent bitterly having set his wife free. He had betrayed her so that now, from his act, she must lead the life of a wild fox for ever, and must undergo all the rigours and hardships of the climate, and all the hazards of a hunted creature. When Mr. Tebrick got back to the cottage he found Mrs. Cork was sitting up for him. It was already late.

'What have you done with Mrs. Tebrick, sir? I missed her, and I missed you, and I have not known what to do, expecting something dreadful had happened. I have been sitting up for you half the night. And where is she now, sir?'

She accosted him so vigorously that Mr. Tebrick stood silent. At length he said: 'I have let her go. She has run away.'

'Poor Miss Silvia!' cried the old woman. 'Poor creature! You ought to be ashamed, sir! Let her go indeed! Poor lady, is that the way for her husband to talk! It is a disgrace. But I saw it coming from the first.'

The old woman was white with fury, she did not mind what she said, but Mr. Tebrick was not listening to her. At last he looked at her and saw that she had just begun to cry, so he went out of the room and up to bed, and lay down as he was, in his clothes, utterly exhausted, and fell into a dog's sleep, starting up every now and then with horror, and then falling back with fatigue. It was late when he woke up, but cold and raw, and he felt cramped in all his limbs. As he lay he heard again the noise which had woken him – the trotting of several horses, and the voices of men riding by the house. Mr. Tebrick jumped up and ran to the window and then looked out, and the first thing that he saw was a gentleman in a pink coat riding at a walk down the lane. At this sight Mr. Tebrick waited no longer, but pulling on his boots in mad haste, ran out instantly, meaning to say that they must not hunt, and how his wife was escaped and they might kill her.

But when he found himself outside the cottage words failed him and fury took possession of him, so that he could only cry out:

'How dare you, you damned blackguard?'

And so, with a stick in his hand, he threw himself on the gentleman in the pink coat and seized his horse's rein, and catching the gentleman by the leg was trying to throw him. But really it is impossible to say what Mr. Tebrick intended by his behaviour or what he would have done, for the gentleman finding himself suddenly assaulted in so unexpected a fashion by so strange a touzled and dishevelled figure, clubbed his hunting crop and dealt him a blow on the temple so that he fell insensible.

Another gentleman rode up at this moment and they were civil enough to dismount and carry Mr. Tebrick into the cottage, where they were met by old Nanny who kept wringing her hands and told them Mr. Tebrick's wife had run away and she was a vixen, and that was the cause that Mr. Tebrick had run out and assaulted them.

The two gentlemen could not help laughing at this, and mounting their horses rode on without delay, after telling each other that Mr. Tebrick, whoever he was, was certainly a madman, and the old woman seemed as mad as her master.

This story, however, went the rounds of the gentry in those

parts and perfectly confirmed everyone in their previous opinion, namely that Mr. Tebrick was mad and his wife had run away from him. The part about her being a vixen was laughed at by the few that heard it, but was soon left out as immaterial to the story, and incredible in itself, though afterwards it came to be remembered and its significance to be understood.

When Mr. Tebrick came to himself it was past noon, and his head was aching so painfully that he could only call to mind in a confused way what had happened.

However, he sent off Mrs. Cork's son directly on one of his horses to enquire about the hunt.

At the same time he gave orders to old Nanny that she was to put out food and water for her mistress, on the chance that she might yet be in the neighbourhood.

By nightfall Simon was back with the news that the hunt had had a very long run but had lost one fox, then, drawing a covert, had chopped an old dog fox, and so ended the day's sport.

This put poor Mr. Tebrick in some hopes again, and he rose at once from his bed, and went out to the wood and began calling his wife, but was overcome with faintness, and lay down and so passed the night in the open, from mere weakness.

In the morning he got back again to the cottage but he had taken a chill, and so had to keep his bed for three or four days after.

All this time he had food put out for her every night, but though rats came to it and ate of it, there were never any prints of a fox.

At last his anxiety began working another way, that is he came to think it possible that his vixen would have gone back to Stokoe, so he had his horses harnessed in the dogcart and brought to the door and then drove over to Rylands, though he was still in a fever, and with a heavy cold upon him.

After that he lived always solitary, keeping away from his fellows and only seeing one man, called Askew, who had been brought up a jockey at Wantage, but was grown too big for his profession. He mounted this loafing fellow on one of his horses three days a week and had him follow the hunt and report to him whenever they killed, and if he could view the fox so much the better, and then he made him describe it minutely, so he should know if it were his Silvia. But he dared not trust himself to go himself, lest his passion should master him and he might commit a murder.

Every time there was a hunt in the neighbourhood he set the gates wide open at Rylands and the house doors also, and taking his gun stood sentinel in the hope that his wife would run in if she were pressed by the hounds, and so he could save her. But only once a hunt came near, when two foxhounds that had lost the main pack strayed on to his land and he shot them instantly and buried them afterwards himself.

It was not long now to the end of the season, as it was the middle of March.

But living as he did at this time, Mr. Tebrick grew more and more to be a true misanthrope. He denied admittance to any that came to visit him, and rarely showed himself to his fellows, but went out chiefly in the early mornings before people were about, in the hope of seeing his beloved fox. Indeed it was only this hope that he would see her again that kept him alive, for he had become so careless of his own comfort in every way that he very seldom ate a proper meal, taking no more than a crust of bread with a morsel of cheese in the whole day, though sometimes he would drink half a bottle of whisky to drown his sorrow and to get off to sleep, for sleep fled from him, and no sooner did he begin dozing but he awoke with a start thinking he had heard something. He let his beard grow too, and though he had always been very particular in his person before, he now was utterly careless of it, gave up washing himself for a week or two at a stretch, and if there was dirt under his finger nails let it stop there.

All this disorder fed a malignant pleasure in him. For by now he had come to hate his fellow men and was embittered against all human decencies and decorum. For strange to tell he never once in these months regretted his dear wife whom he had so much loved. No, all that he grieved for now was his departed vixen. He was haunted all this time not by the memory of a sweet and gentle woman, but by the recollection of an animal; a beast it is true that could sit at table and play piquet when it would, but for all that nothing really but a wild beast. His one hope now was the recovery of this beast, and of this he dreamed continually. Likewise both waking and sleeping he was visited by visions of her; her mask, her full white-tagged brush, white throat, and the thick fur in her ears all haunted him.

Every one of her foxey ways was now so absolutely precious to him that I believe that if he had known for certain she was dead, and had thoughts of marrying a second time, he would never have been happy with a woman. No, indeed, he would have been more tempted to get himself a tame fox, and would have counted that as good a marriage as he could make.

Yet this all proceeded one may say from a passion, and a true conjugal fidelity, that it would be hard to find matched in this world. And though we may think him a fool, almost a madman, we must, when we look closer, find much to respect in his extraordinary devotion. How different indeed was he from those who, if their wives go mad, shut them in madhouses and give themselves up to concubinage, and nay, what is more, there are many who extenuate such conduct too. But Mr. Tebrick was of a very different temper, and though his wife was now nothing but a hunted beast, cared for no one in the world but her.

But this devouring love ate into him like a consumption, so that by sleepless nights, and not caring for his person, in a few months he was worn to the shadow of himself. His cheeks were sunk in, his eyes hollow but excessively brilliant, and his whole body had lost flesh, so that looking at him the wonder was that he was still alive.

Now that the hunting season was over he had less anxiety for her, yet even so he was not positive that the hounds had not got her. For between the time of his setting her free, and the end of the hunting season (just after Easter), there were

117

but three vixens killed near. Of those three one was a half-blind or wall-eyed, and one was a very grey dull-coloured beast. The third answered more to the description of his wife, but that it had not much black on the legs, whereas in her the blackness of the legs was very plain to be noticed. But yet his fear made him think that perhaps she had got mired in running and the legs being muddy were not remarked on as black.

One morning the first week in May, about four o'clock, when he was out waiting in the little copse, he sat down for a while on a tree stump, and when he looked up saw a fox coming towards him over the ploughed field. It was carrying a hare over its shoulder so that it was nearly all hidden from him. At last, when it was not twenty yards from him, it crossed over, going into the copse, when Mr. Tebrick stood up and cried out, 'Silvia, Silvia, is it you?'

The fox dropped the hare out of his mouth and stood looking at him, and then our gentleman saw at the first glance that this was not his wife. For whereas Mrs. Tebrick had been of a very bright red, this was a swarthier duller beast altogether, moreover it was a good deal larger and higher at the shoulder and had a great white tag to his brush. But the fox after the first instant did not stand for his portrait you may be sure, but picked up his hare and made off like an arrow.

Then Mr. Tebrick cried out to himself: 'Indeed I am crazy now! My affliction has made me lose what little reason I ever had. Here am I taking every fox I see to be my wife! My neighbours call me a madman and now I see that they are right. Look at me now, oh God! How foul a creature I am. I hate my fellows. I am thin and wasted by this consuming passion, my reason is gone and I feed myself on dreams. Recall me to my duty, bring me back to decency, let me not become a beast likewise, but restore me and forgive me, Oh my Lord.'

With that he burst into scalding tears and knelt down and prayed, a thing he had not done for many weeks.

When he rose up he walked back feeling giddy and

exceedingly weak, but with a contrite heart, and then washed himself thoroughly and changed his clothes, but his weakness increasing he lay down for the rest of the day, but read in the Book of Job and was much comforted.

For several days after this he lived very soberly, for his weakness continued, but every day he read in the Bible, and prayed earnestly, so that his resolution was so much strengthened that he determined to overcome his folly, or his passion, if he could, and at any rate to live the rest of his life very religiously. So strong was this desire in him to amend his ways that he considered if he should not go to spread the Gospel abroad, for the Bible Society, and so spend the rest of his days.

Indeed he began a letter to his wife's uncle, the canon, and he was writing this when he was startled by hearing a fox bark.

Yet so great was this new turn he had taken that he did not rush out at once, as he would have done before, but stayed where he was and finished his letter.

Afterwards he said to himself that it was only a wild fox and sent by the devil to mock him, and that madness lay that way if he should listen. But on the other hand he could not deny to himself that it might have been his wife, and that he ought to welcome the prodigal. Thus he was torn between these two thoughts, neither of which did he completely believe. He stayed thus tormented with doubts and fears all night.

The next morning he woke suddenly with a start and on the instant heard a fox bark once more. At that he pulled on his clothes and ran out as fast as he could to the garden gate. The sun was not yet high, the dew thick everywhere, and for a minute or two everything was very silent. He looked about him eagerly but could see no fox, yet there was already joy in his heart.

Then while he looked up and down the road, he saw his vixen step out of the copse about thirty yards away. He called to her at once.

'My dearest wife! Oh, Silvia! You are come back!' and at

the sound of his voice he saw her wag her tail, which set his last doubts at rest.

But then though he called her again, she stepped into the copse once more though she looked back at him over her shoulder as she went. At this he ran after her, but softly and not too fast lest he should frighten her away, and then looked about for her again and called to her when he saw her among the trees still keeping her distance from him. He followed her then, and as he approached so she retreated from him, yet always looking back at him several times.

He followed after her through the underwood up the side of the hill, when suddenly she disappeared from his sight, behind some bracken.

When he got there he could see her nowhere, but looking about him found a fox's earth, but so well hidden that he might have passed it by a thousand times and would never have found it unless he had made particular search at that spot.

But now, though he went on his hands and knees, he could see nothing of his vixen, so that he waited a little while wondering.

Presently he heard a noise of something moving in the earth, and so waited silently, then saw something which pushed itself into sight. It was a small sooty black beast, like a puppy. There came another behind it, then another and so on till there were five of them. Lastly there came his vixen pushing her litter before her, and while he looked at her silently, a prey to his confused and unhappy emotions, he saw that her eyes were shining with pride and happiness.

She picked up one of her youngsters then, in her mouth, and brought it to him and laid it in front of him, and then looked up at him very excited, or so it seemed.

Mr. Tebrick took the cub in his hands, stroked it and put it against his cheek. It was a little fellow with a smutty face and paws, with staring vacant eyes of a brilliant electric blue and a little tail like a carrot. When he was put down he took a step towards his mother and then sat down very comically.

Mr. Tebrick looked at his wife again and spoke to her,

calling her a good creature. Already he was resigned and now, indeed, for the first time he thoroughly understood what had happened to her, and how far apart they were now. But looking first at one cub, then at another, and having them sprawling over his lap, he forgot himself, only watching the pretty scene, and taking pleasure in it. Now and then he would stroke his vixen and kiss her, liberties which she freely allowed him. He marvelled more than ever now at her beauty; for her gentleness with the cubs and the extreme delight she took in them seemed to him then to make her more lovely than before. Thus lying amongst them at the mouth of the earth he idled away the whole of the morning.

First he would play with one, then with another, rolling them over and tickling them, but they were too young yet to lend themselves to any other more active sport than this. Every now and then he would stroke his vixen, or look at her, and thus the time slipped away quite fast and he was surprised when she gathered her cubs together and pushed them before her into the earth, then coming back to him once or twice very humanly bid him 'Good-bye and that she hoped she would see him soon again, now he had found out the way.'

So admirably did she express her meaning that it would have been superfluous for her to have spoken had she been able, and Mr. Tebrick, who was used to her, got up at once and went home.

But now that he was alone, all the feelings which he had not troubled himself with when he was with her, but had, as

it were, put aside till after his innocent pleasures were over, all these came swarming back to assail him in a hundred tormenting ways.

Firstly he asked himself: Was not his wife unfaithful to him, had she not prostituted herself to a beast? Could he still love her after that? But this did not trouble him so much as it might have done. For now he was convinced inwardly that she could no longer in fairness be judged as a woman, but as a fox only. And as a fox she had done no more than other foxes, indeed in having cubs and tending them with love, she had done well.

Whether in this conclusion Mr. Tebrick was in the right or not, is not for us here to consider. But I would only say to those who would censure him for a too lenient view of the religious side of the matter, that we have not seen the thing as he did, and perhaps if it were displayed before our eyes we might be led to the same conclusions.

This was, however, not a tenth part of the trouble in which Mr. Tebrick found himself. For he asked himself also: 'Was I not jealous?' And looking into his heart he found that he was indeed jealous, yes, and angry too, that now he must share his vixen with wild foxes. Then he questioned himself if it were not dishonourable to do so, and whether he should not utterly forget her and follow his original intention of retiring from the world, and see her no more.

Thus he tormented himself for the rest of that day, and by evening he had resolved never to see her again.

But in the middle of the night he woke up with his head very clear, and said to himself in wonder, 'Am I not a madman? I torment myself foolishly with fantastic notions. Can a man have his honour sullied by a beast? I am a man, I am immeasurably superior to the animals. Can my dignity allow of my being jealous of a beast? A thousand times no. Were I to lust after a vixen, I were a criminal indeed. I can be happy in seeing my vixen, for I love her, but she does right to be happy according to the laws of her being.'

Lastly, he said to himself what was, he felt, the truth of this whole matter:

'When I am with her I am happy. But now I distort what is simple and drive myself crazy with false reasoning upon it.'

Yet before he slept again he prayed, but though he had thought first to pray for guidance, in reality he prayed only that on the morrow he would see his vixen again and that God would preserve her, and her cubs too, from all dangers, and would allow him to see them often, so that he might come to love them for her sake as if he were their father, and that if this were a sin he might be forgiven, for he sinned in ignorance.

The next day or two he saw vixen and cubs again, though his visits were cut shorter, and these visits gave him such an innocent pleasure that very soon his notions of honour, duty and so on, were entirely forgotten, and his jealousy lulled asleep.

One day he tried taking with him the stereoscope and a pack of cards.

But though his Silvia was affectionate and amiable enough to let him put the stereoscope over her muzzle, yet she would not look through it, but kept turning her head to lick his hand, and it was plain to him that now she had quite forgotten the use of the instrument. It was the same too with the cards. For with them she was pleased enough, but only delighting to bite at them, and flip them about with her paws, and never considering for a moment whether they were diamonds or clubs, or hearts, or spades or whether the card was an ace or not. So it was evident that she had forgotten the nature of cards too.

Thereafter he only brought them things which she could better enjoy, that is sugar, grapes, raisins, and butcher's meat.

By-and-bye, as the summer wore on, the cubs came to know him, and he them, so that he was able to tell them easily apart, and then he christened them. For this purpose he brought a little bowl of water, sprinkled them as if in baptism and told them he was their godfather and gave each of them a name, calling them Sorel, Kasper, Selwyn, Esther, and Angelica.

Sorel was a clumsy little beast of a cheery and indeed puppyish disposition; Kasper was fierce, the largest of the five, even in his play he would always bite, and gave his godfather many a sharp nip as time went on. Esther was of a dark complexion, a true brunette and very sturdy; Angelica the brightest red and the most exactly like her mother; while Selwyn was the smallest cub, of a very prying, inquisitive and cunning temper, but delicate and undersized.

Thus Mr. Tebrick had a whole family now to occupy him, and, indeed, came to love them with very much of a father's love and partiality.

His favourite was Angelica (who reminded him so much of her mother in her pretty ways) because of a gentleness which was lacking in the others, even in their play. After her in his affections came Selwyn, whom he soon saw was the most intelligent of the whole litter. Indeed he was so much more quick-witted than the rest that Mr. Tebrick was led into speculating as to whether he had not inherited something of the human from his dam. Thus very early he learnt to know his name, and would come when he was called, and what was

stranger still, he learnt the names of his brothers and sisters before they came to do so themselves.

Besides all this he was something of a young philosopher, for though his brother Kasper tyrannized over him he put up with it all with an unruffled temper. He was not, however, above playing tricks on the others, and one day when Mr. Tebrick was by, he made believe that there was a mouse in a hole some little way off. Very soon he was joined by Sorel, and presently by Kasper and Esther. When he had got them all digging, it was easy for him to slip away, and then he came to his godfather with a sly look, sat down before him, and smiled and then jerked his head over towards the others and smiled again and wrinkled his brows so that Mr. Tebrick knew as well as if he had spoken that the youngster was saying, 'Have I not made fools of them all?'

He was the only one that was curious about Mr. Tebrick: he made him take out his watch, put his ear to it, considered it and wrinkled up his brows in perplexity. On the next visit it was the same thing. He must see the watch again, and again think over it. But clever as he was, little Selwyn could never understand it, and if his mother remembered anything about watches it was a subject which she never attempted to explain to her children.

One day Mr. Tebrick left the earth as usual and ran down the slope to the road, when he was surprised to find a carriage waiting before his house and a coachman walking about near his gate. Mr. Tebrick went in and found that his visitor was waiting for him. It was his wife's uncle.

They shook hands, though the Rev. Canon Fox did not recognise him immediately, and Mr. Tebrick led him into the house.

The clergyman looked about him a good deal, at the dirty and disorderly rooms, and when Mr. Tebrick took him into the drawing room it was evident that it had been unused for several months, the dust lay so thickly on all the furniture.

After some conversation on indifferent topics Canon Fox said to him:

'I have called really to ask about my niece.'

Mr. Tebrick was silent for some time and then said:

'She is quite happy now.'

'Ah – indeed. I have heard she is not living with you any longer.'

'No. She is not living with me. She is not far away. I see her every day now.'

'Indeed. Where does she live?'

'In the woods with her children. I ought to tell you that she has changed her shape. She is a fox.'

The Rev. Canon Fox got up; he was alarmed, and everything Mr. Tebrick said confirmed what he had been led to expect he would find at Rylands. When he was outside, however, he asked Mr. Tebrick:

'You don't have many visitors now, eh?'

'No – I never see anyone if I can avoid it. You are the first person I have spoken to for months.'

'Quite right, too, my dear fellow. I quite understand – in the circumstances.' Then the cleric shook him by the hand, got into his carriage and drove away.

'At any rate,' he said to himself, 'there will be no scandal.' He was relieved also because Mr. Tebrick had said nothing about going abroad to disseminate the Gospel. Canon Fox had been alarmed by the letter, had not answered it, and thought that it was always better to let things be, and never to refer to anything unpleasant. He did not at all want to recommend Mr. Tebrick to the Bible Society if he were mad. His eccentricities would never be noticed at Stokoe. Besides that, Mr. Tebrick had said he was happy.

He was sorry for Mr. Tebrick too, and he said to himself that the queer girl, his niece, must have married him because he was the first man she had met. He reflected also that he was never likely to see her again and said aloud, when he had driven some little way:

'Not an affectionate disposition,' then to his coachman: 'No, that's all right. Drive on, Hopkins.'

When Mr. Tebrick was alone he rejoiced exceedingly in his solitary life. He understood, or so he fancied, what it was to be happy, and that he had found complete happiness now, living from day to day, careless of the future, surrounded every morning by playful and affectionate little creatures whom he loved tenderly, and sitting beside their mother, whose simple happiness was the source of his own.

'True happiness,' he said to himself, 'is to be found in bestowing love; there is no such happiness as that of the mother for her babe, unless I have attained it in mine for my vixen and her children.'

With these feelings he waited impatiently for the hour on the morrow when he might hasten to them once more.

When, however, he had toiled up the hillside, to the earth, taking infinite precaution not to tread down the bracken, or make a beaten path which might lead others to that secret spot, he found to his surprise that Silvia was not there and that there were no cubs to be seen either. He called to them, but it was in vain, and at last he laid himself on the mossy bank beside the earth and waited.

For a long while, as it seemed to him, he lay very still, with closed eyes, straining his ears to hear every rustle among the leaves, or any sound that might be the cubs stirring in the earth.

At last he must have dropped asleep, for he woke suddenly with all his senses alert, and opening his eyes found a full-grown fox within six feet of him sitting on its haunches like a dog and watching his face with curiosity. Mr. Tebrick saw instantly that it was not Silvia. When he moved the fox got up and shifted his eyes, but still stood his ground, and Mr. Tebrick recognised him then for the dog-fox he had seen once before carrying a hare. It was the same dark beast with a large white tag to his brush. Now the secret was out and Mr. Tebrick could see his rival before him. Here was the real father of his godchildren, who could be certain of their taking after him, and leading over again his wild and rakish life. Mr. Tebrick stared for a long time at the handsome rogue, who glanced back at him with distrust and watchfulness patent in his face, but not without defiance too, and it seemed to Mr. Tebrick as if there was also a touch of cynical humour in his look, as if he said:

'By Gad! we two have been strangely brought together!'

And to the man, at any rate, it seemed strange that they were thus linked, and he wondered if the love his rival there bore to his vixen and his cubs were the same thing in kind as his own.

'We would both of us give our lives for theirs,' he said to himself as he reasoned upon it, 'we both of us are happy chiefly in their company. What pride this fellow must feel to have such a wife, and such children taking after him. And has he not reason for his pride? He lives in a world where he is beset with a thousand dangers. For half the year he is hunted, everywhere dogs pursue him, men lay traps for him or menace him. He owes nothing to another.'

But he did not speak, knowing that his words would only alarm the fox; then in a few minutes he saw the dog-fox look over his shoulder, and then he trotted off as lightly as a gossamer veil blown in the wind, and, in a minute or two more, back he comes with his vixen and the cubs all around him. Seeing the dog-fox thus surrounded by vixen and cubs was too much for Mr. Tebrick; in spite of all his philosophy a pang of jealousy shot through him. He could see that Silvia had been hunting with her cubs, and also that she had forgotten that he would come that morning, for she started when she saw him, and though she carelessly licked his hand, he could see that her thoughts were not with him.

Very soon she led her cubs into the earth, the dog-fox had vanished and Mr. Tebrick was again alone. He did not wait longer but went home.

Now was his peace of mind all gone, the happiness which he had flattered himself the night before he knew so well how to enjoy, seemed now but a fool's paradise in which he had been living. A hundred times this poor gentleman bit his lip, drew down his torvous brows, and stamped his foot, and cursed himself bitterly, or called his lady bitch. He could not forgive himself neither, that he had not thought of the damned dog-fox before, but all the while had let the cubs frisk round him, each one a proof that a dog-fox had been at work with his vixen. Yes, jealousy was now in the wind, and every circumstance which had been a reason for his felicity the night before was now turned into a monstrous feature of his nightmare. With all this Mr. Tebrick so worked upon himself that for the time being he had lost his reason. Black was white and white black, and he was resolved that on the morrow he would dig the vile brood of foxes out and shoot them, and so free himself at last from this hellish plague.

All that night he was in this mood, and in agony, as if he had broken in the crown of a tooth and bitten on the nerve. But as all things will have an ending so at last Mr. Tebrick, worn out and wearied by this loathed passion of jealousy, fell into an uneasy and tormented sleep.

After an hour or two the procession of confused and jumbled images which first assailed him passed away and subsided into one clear and powerful dream. His wife was with him in her own proper shape, walking as they had been on that fatal day before her transformation. Yet she was changed too, for in her face there were visible tokens of unhappiness, her face swollen with crying, pale and downcast, her hair hanging in disorder, her damp hands wringing a small handkerchief into a ball, her whole body shaken with sobs, and an air of long neglect about her person. Between her sobs she was confessing to him some crime which she had committed, but he did not catch the broken words, nor did he wish to hear them, for he was dulled by his sorrow. So they continued walking together in sadness as it were for ever, he with his arm about her waist, she turning her head to him and often casting her eyes down in distress.

At last they sat down, and he spoke, saying: 'I know they are not my children, but I shall not use them barbarously because of that. You are still my wife. I swear to you they shall never be neglected. I will pay for their education.'

Then he began turning over the names of schools in his mind. Eton would not do, nor Harrow, nor Winchester, nor Rugby . . . But he could not tell why these schools would not do for these children of hers, he only knew that every school he thought of was impossible, but surely one could be found. So turning over the names of schools he sat for a long while holding his dear wife's hand, till at length, still weeping, she got up and went away and then slowly he awoke.

But even when he had opened his eyes and looked about him he was thinking of schools, saying to himself that he must send them to a private academy, or even at the worst engage a tutor. 'Why, yes,' he said to himself, putting one foot out of bed, 'that is what it must be, a tutor, though even then there will be a difficulty at first.'

At those words he wondered what difficulty there would be and recollected that they were not ordinary children. No, they were foxes – mere foxes. When poor Mr. Tebrick had remembered this he was, as it were, dazed or stunned by the fact, and for a long time he could understand nothing, but at last burst into a flood of tears compassionating them and himself too. The awfulness of the fact itself, that his dear wife should have foxes instead of children, filled him with an agony of pity, and, at length, when he recollected the cause of their being foxes, that is that his wife was a fox also, his tears broke out anew, and he could bear it no longer but began calling out in his anguish, and beat his head once or twice against the wall, and then cast himself down on his bed again and wept and wept, sometimes tearing the sheets asunder with his teeth.

The whole of that day, for he was not to go to the earth till evening, he went about sorrowfully, torn by true pity for his poor vixen and her children.

At last when the time came he went again up to the earth, which he found deserted, but hearing his voice, out came Esther. But though he called the others by their names there was no answer, and something in the way the cub greeted him made him fancy she was indeed alone. She was truly rejoiced to see him, and scrambled up into his arms, and thence to his shoulder, kissing him, which was unusual in her (though natural enough in her sister Angelica). He sat down a little way from the earth fondling her, and fed her with some fish he had brought for her mother, which she ate so ravenously that he concluded she must have been short of food that day and probably alone for some time.

130

At last while he was sitting there Esther pricked up her ears, started up, and presently Mr. Tebrick saw his vixen come towards them. She greeted him very affectionately but it was plain had not much time to spare, for she soon started back whence she had come with Esther at her side. When they had gone about a rod the cub hung back and kept stopping and looking back to the earth, and at last turned and ran back home. But her mother was not to be fobbed off so, for she quickly overtook her child and gripping her by the scruff began to drag her along with her.

Mr. Tebrick, seeing then how matters stood, spoke to her, telling her he would carry Esther if she would lead, so after a little while Silvia gave her over, and then they set out on their strange journey.

Silvia went running on a little before while Mr. Tebrick followed after with Esther in his arms whimpering and struggling now to be free, and indeed, once she gave him a nip with her teeth. This was not so strange a thing to him now, and he knew the remedy for it, which is much the same as with others whose tempers run too high, that is a taste of it themselves. Mr. Tebrick shook her and gave her a smart little cuff, after which, though she sulked, she stopped her biting.

They went thus above a mile, circling his house and crossing the highway until they gained a small covert that lay with some waste fields adjacent to it. And by this time it was so dark that it was all Mr. Tebrick could do to pick his way, for it was not always easy for him to follow where his vixen found a big enough road for herself.

But at length they came to another earth, and by the

starlight Mr. Tebrick could just make out the other cubs skylarking in the shadows.

Now he was tired, but he was happy and laughed softly for joy, and presently his vixen, coming to him, put her feet upon his shoulders as he sat on the ground, and licked him, and he kissed her back on the muzzle and gathered her in his arms and rolled her in his jacket and then laughed and wept by turns in the excess of his joy.

All his jealousies of the night before were forgotten now. All his desperate sorrow of the morning and the horror of his dream were gone. What if they were foxes? Mr. Tebrick found that he could be happy with them. As the weather was hot he lay out there all the night, first playing hide and seek with them in the dark till, missing his vixen and the cubs proving obstreperous, he lay down and was soon asleep.

He was woken up soon after dawn by one of the cubs tugging at his shoelaces in play. When he sat up he saw two of the cubs standing near him on their hind legs, wrestling with each other, the other two were playing hide and seek round a tree trunk, and now Angelica let go his laces and came romping into his arms to kiss him and say 'Good morning' to him, then worrying the points of his waistcoat a little shyly after the warmth of his embrace.

That moment of awakening was very sweet to him. The freshness of the morning, the scent of everything at the day's rebirth, the first beams of the sun upon a tree-top near, and a pigeon rising into the air suddenly, all delighted him. Even the rough scent of the body of the cub in his arms seemed to him delicious.

At that moment all human customs and institutions seemed to him nothing but folly; for said he, 'I would exchange all my life as a man for my happiness now, and even now I retain almost all of the ridiculous conceptions of a man. The beasts are happier and I will deserve that happiness as best I can.'

After he had looked at the cubs playing merrily, how, with soft stealth, one would creep behind another to bounce out and startle him, a thought came into Mr. Tebrick's head, and that was that these cubs were innocent, they were as stainless snow, they could not sin, for God had created them to be thus and they could break none of His commandments. And he fancied also that men sin because they cannot be as the animals.

Presently he got up full of happiness, and began making his way home when suddenly he came to a full stop and asked himself: 'What is going to happen to them?'

This question rooted him stockishly in a cold and deadly fear as if he had seen a snake before him. At last he shook his head and hurried on his path. Aye, indeed, what would become of his vixen and her children?

This thought put him into such a fever of apprehension that he did his best not to think of it any more, but yet it stayed with him all that day and for weeks after, at the back of his mind, so that he was not careless in his happiness as before, but as it were trying continually to escape his own thoughts.

This made him also anxious to pass all the time he could with his dear Silvia, and, therefore, he began going out to them for more of the daytime, and then he would sleep the night in the woods also as he had done that night; and so he passed several weeks, only returning to his house occasionally to get himself a fresh provision of food. But after a week or ten days at the new earth both his vixen and the cubs, too, got a new habit of roaming. For a long while back, as he knew, his vixen had been lying out alone most of the day, and now the cubs were all for doing the same thing. The earth, in short, had served its purpose and was now distasteful to them, and they would not enter it unless pressed with fear.

This new manner of their lives was an added grief to Mr. Tebrick, for sometimes he missed them for hours together, or for the whole day even, and not knowing where they might be was lonely and anxious. Yet his Silvia was thoughtful for him too and would often send Angelica or another of the cubs to fetch him to their new lair, or come herself if she could spare the time. For now they were all perfectly accustomed to his presence, and had come to look on him as their natural companion, and although he was in many ways irksome to them by scaring rabbits, yet they always rejoiced to see him when they had been parted from him. This friendliness of theirs was, you may be sure, the source of most of Mr. Tebrick's happiness at this time. Indeed he lived now for nothing but his foxes, his love for his vixen had extended itself insensibly to include her cubs, and these were now his daily playmates so that he knew them as well as if they had been his own children. With Selwyn and Angelica indeed he was always happy; and they never so much as when they were with him. He was not stiff in his behaviour either, but had learnt by this time as much from his foxes as they had from him. Indeed never was there a more curious alliance than this or one with stranger effects upon both of the parties.

Mr. Tebrick now could follow after them anywhere and keep up with them too, and could go through a wood as silently as a deer. He learnt to conceal himself if ever a labourer passed by so that he was rarely seen, and never but once in their company. But what was most strange of all, he had got a way of going doubled up, often almost on all fours with his hands touching the ground every now and then, particularly when he went uphill.

He hunted with them too sometimes, chiefly by coming up and scaring rabbits towards where the cubs lay ambushed, so that the bunnies ran straight into their jaws.

He was useful to them in other ways, climbing up and robbing pigeon's nests for the eggs which they relished exceedingly, or by occasionally dispatching a hedgehog for them so they did not get the prickles in their mouths. But while on his part he thus altered his conduct, they on their side were not behindhand, but learnt a dozen human tricks from him that are ordinarily wanting in Reynard's education.

One evening he went to a cottager who had a row of skeps, and bought one of them, just as it was after the man had smothered the bees. This he carried to the foxes that they might taste the honey, for he had seen them dig out wild bees' nests often enough. The skep full was indeed a wonderful feast for them, they bit greedily into the heavy scented comb, their jaws were drowned in the sticky flood of sweetness, and

they gorged themselves on it without restraint. When they had crunched up the last morsel they tore the skep in pieces, and for hours afterwards they were happily employed in licking themselves clean.

That night he slept near their lair, but they left him and went hunting. In the morning when he woke he was quite numb with cold, and faint with hunger. A white mist hung over everything and the wood smelt of autumn.

He got up and stretched his cramped limbs, and then walked homewards. The summer was over and Mr. Tebrick noticed this now for the first time and was astonished. He reflected that the cubs were fast growing up, they were foxes at all points, and yet when he thought of the time when they had been sooty and had blue eyes it seemed to him only yesterday. From that he passed to thinking of the future, asking himself as he had done once before what would become of his vixen and her children. Before the winter he must tempt them into the security of his garden, and fortify it against all the dangers that threatened them.

But though he tried to allay his fear with such resolutions

he remained uneasy all that day. When he went out to them that afternoon he found only his wife Silvia there and it was plain to him that she too was alarmed, but alas, poor creature, she could tell him nothing, only lick his hands and face, and turn about pricking her ears at every sound.

'Where are your children, Silvia?' he asked her several times, but she was impatient of his questions, but at last sprang into his arms, flattened herself upon his breast and kissed him gently, so that when he departed his heart was lighter because he knew that she still loved him.

That night he slept indoors, but in the morning early he was awoken by the sound of trotting horses, and running to the window saw a farmer riding by very sprucely dressed. Could they be hunting so soon, he wondered, but presently reassured himself that it could not be a hunt already.

He heard no other sound till eleven o'clock in the morning when suddenly there was the clamour of hounds giving tongue and not so far off neither. At this Mr. Tebrick ran out of his house distracted and set open the gates of his garden, but with iron bars and wire at the top so the huntsmen could not follow. There was silence again; it seems the fox must have turned away, for there was no other sound of the hunt. Mr. Tebrick was now like one helpless with fear, he dared not go out, yet could not stay still at home. There was nothing that he could do, yet he would not admit this, so he busied himself in making holes in the hedges, so that Silvia (or her cubs) could enter from whatever side she came.

At last he forced himself to go indoors and sit down and drink some tea. While he was there he fancied he heard the hounds again; it was but a faint ghostly echo of their music, yet when he ran out of the house it was already close at hand in the copse above.

Now it was that poor Mr. Tebrick made his great mistake, for hearing the hounds almost outside the gate he ran to meet them, whereas rightly he should have run back to the house. As soon as he reached the gate he saw his wife Silvia coming towards him but very tired with running and just upon her the hounds. The horror of that sight pierced him, for ever afterwards he was haunted by those hounds – their eagerness, their desperate efforts to gain on her, and their blind lust for her came at odd moments to frighten him all his life. Now he should have run back, though it was already late, but instead he cried out to her, and she ran straight through the open gate to him. What followed was all over in a flash, but it was seen by many witnesses.

The side of Mr. Tebrick's garden there is bounded by a wall, about six feet high and curving round, so that the huntsmen could see over this wall inside. One of them indeed put his horse at it very boldly, which was risking his neck, and although he got over safe was too late to be of much assistance.

His vixen had at once sprung into Mr. Tebrick's arms, and before he could turn back the hounds were upon them and had pulled them down. Then at that moment there was a scream of despair heard by all the field that had come up, which they declared afterwards was more like a woman's voice than a man's. But yet there was no clear proof whether it was Mr. Tebrick or his wife who had suddenly regained her voice. When the huntsman who had leapt the wall got to them and had whipped off the hounds Mr. Tebrick had been terribly mauled and was bleeding from twenty wounds. As for his vixen she was dead, though he was still clasping her dead body in his arms.

Mr. Tebrick was carried into the house at once and assistance sent for, but there was no doubt now about his neighbours being in the right when they called him mad.

For a long while his life was despaired of, but at last he rallied, and in the end he recovered his reason and lived to be a great age, for that matter he is still alive.